Bridgers

A Parable

Angie Thompson

Quiet Waters Press
Lynchburg, Virginia

Copyright © 2018 by Angie Thompson

First published November 2017

All rights reserved. No portion of this book may be reproduced in any form without permission from the publisher, except as permitted by U.S. copyright law. For permissions, email: contact@quietwaterspress.com

Cover illustration by Susanitah, licensed through Shutterstock.com
Sheep logo adapted from original at PublicDomainPictures.net
Scripture taken from the New King James Version. ©1982 by Thomas Nelson, Inc. Used by permission. All rights reserved.

This is a work of fiction. Names, characters, places, and incidents are the products of the author's imagination or are used fictitiously. Any resemblance to actual events, locales, or persons, living or dead, is entirely coincidental.

ISBN: 978-0-9996144-0-2 (pbk)
ISBN: 978-0-9996144-1-9 (ePub)

Publisher's Cataloging-in-Publication data

Names: Thompson, Angie, author.
Title: Bridgers: a parable / by Angie Thompson.
Description: Lynchburg, Virginia : Quiet Waters Press, 2017. | Summary: In a modern retelling of the Good Samaritan parable, a deeply divided community receives a shock when an unlikely hero steps in to help a victim of a violent crime. | Audience: Ages 14 and up.
Identifiers: ISBN 9780999614402 (softcover) | ISBN 9780999614419 (epub)
Subjects: LCSH: Good Samaritan (Parable)–Fiction. | Christian Life–Fiction. | Friendship–Fiction. | BISAC: YOUNG ADULT FICTION / Religious / Christian / General.
Classification: LCC PZ7.1.T4677 Br 2017

*For Grandpa, who always wanted
to see one of my stories in print*

Parents' Note

As an advanced reader from an early age, I understand the struggles of these children and their parents in finding books that are both challenging and free of inappropriate content. My goal has always been to write stories that are safe, not only for a teen audience, but also for younger children with the reading skills to enjoy and appreciate them.

Because of the nature of the parable that inspired this book, it contains references to topics that may be inappropriate for younger readers. Drinking, gangs, and drugs are mentioned but not described. A main character smokes cigarettes, and this issue is partially addressed in a later scene. Tattoos are not specifically condemned but are shown to make others uncomfortable. The aftermath of a violent crime is described, but not in a graphic manner.

Parents may want to preview the book or discuss these issues when giving it to a younger child.

Table of Contents

Chapter One 1
Chapter Two 5
Chapter Three 9
Chapter Four 13
Chapter Five 17
Chapter Six 19
Chapter Seven 21
Chapter Eight 25
Chapter Nine 27
Chapter Ten 31
Chapter Eleven 35
Chapter Twelve 39
Chapter Thirteen 43
Chapter Fourteen 47
Chapter Fifteen 51
Chapter Sixteen 55
Chapter Seventeen 59
Chapter Eighteen 63
Chapter Nineteen 67
Chapter Twenty 73
Chapter Twenty-One 77
Chapter Twenty-Two 83
Chapter Twenty-Three 87
Chapter Twenty-Four 91
Chapter Twenty-Five 95
Chapter Twenty-Six 99
Chapter Twenty-Seven 103
Chapter Twenty-Eight 107
Chapter Twenty-Nine 111
Chapter Thirty 115
Chapter Thirty-One 119
Chapter Thirty-Two 125

Chapter One

I'm glad the guy's probably dead by now, because if I ever met him, I'd punch him in the face.

I'd never say that at school—the only place I ever think it. It's the kind of thing that'd draw attention from teachers and counselors, Principal Orbison and Officer Clay—people that'd never put a face to the name DaVonte Jones unless they thought I'd make trouble. I guess I look like the kid you wouldn't want to meet in a dark alley, and they'd figure I'd really do it.

The guys from my neighborhood would get a kick out of it. I've never hit anybody unless they were hurting a little kid, and when I get mad, a couple jabs at what's left of the punching bag in the corner of the old rec center usually cools me down. But I look like I could do it, and that's what counts to most people.

The tattoos—sure, they could be intimidating, I guess. But there aren't any gang symbols. Just pictures I thought were cool, style statements that don't look like someone else's trash, proof to the guys on the block that I belong, even if I keep out of some of the garbage they're into.

The cigarettes—well, I dare anyone to live in my neighborhood for sixteen years and not at least try them. I don't use them as much as some guys, but they're a big help when I get stressed. Besides, I've never seen anyone passed out in the street or whacked out of their mind from a cigarette, so I figure they can't be that bad.

And the way I dress—yeah, let's just say I'd been wearing ripped jeans and frayed shirts long before somebody made them cool. Most of the money I get from my mama when she's sober goes to more important things like school lunches or frozen dinners. And even if I could afford it, walking down my street in a collared shirt would just be begging for the fights I'd rather avoid.

I don't even know the guy's name, and I guess he might've meant all right, but I can tell you one thing—he wasn't from Graveside. Because anyone from this side of the river would've known right off that bussing the kids from my neighborhood over to Woodbridge High would be the worst idea in the history of the city.

The names haven't changed much in forty years. The rich kids call us deadbeats, which might be just a slap at our future or a dig at the cemetery where our neighborhood got its name. To us, they're the bridgers, either because half of them live in Woodbridge or because you have to cross the bridge to get to them. That name's the deepest insult you can give a Graveside kid.

Why nobody on the school board ever redrew the lines again after that disaster is one of life's unsolved mysteries. Nobody, but nobody wants the Graveside kids in this school—least of all us. Most days we pretty much manage to ignore each other, but some days we just can't. Days like today, when Pete Hoffstedder and Ian LeBeau filled Jamal Lewis's gym sneakers with some sort of rotten-smelling muck while he was in the shower.

Jamal shoved Ian up against a locker and ended up with a black eye from Pete and two weeks' suspension from the principal. Ian and Pete got three days' detention and had to pay damages—a whopping ten bucks. Maybe Mr. Orbison never had to replace a pair of sneakers, no matter how torn-up they were.

The rest of the day was electric. Guys jostled and pushed in the halls. Girls shot poison looks across the classrooms. Teachers scrapped group work and lectured with tight lips, keeping a worried eye on the Graveside kids and nervously shushing the whispered digs of the bridgers.

I guess it's a little like living over an ammunition plant. After forty years, nobody expects an explosion, but everyone still catches their breath when a lit cigarette falls on the floor. Next week, it'll all be back to normal, just with one more inch carved into the gap that separates us. And as far as I can see, that's a gap no bridge in the world will ever cross.

Chapter Two

"Two weeks! They should've kicked him out for good." Peyton Emeric scowled at his friend's face on the phone as he sprawled across his bed. "You ought to have your parents appeal to the school board. Ten bucks? He couldn't have given those shoes away. They were pretty much held together with duct tape. You were doing him a favor."

He paused, listening to his earbuds, then shook his head.

"Nah, I can't. Church stuff tonight. So what'd the doctor say?"

Another pause, and Peyton's scowl deepened.

"I mean, can't you make the kid's insurance pay for bruises? Pain and suffering or something? I'm telling you, your dad should check it out. There's got to be some sort of assault there. Maybe send him to jail if you can't get money out of it. Those kids are dangerous. Somebody has to teach them a lesson."

"Peyton?" A soft knock interrupted Ian's reply, and his friend glanced up irritably.

"I'm busy, Natalie!"

"Phone for you. It's Pastor Allison."

Peyton sat up and shook his hair back into place as he reached for his phone.

"Hey, listen, I have to go. Think about it. I'll see you tomorrow."

He pulled off the earbuds, tossed the phone back onto the bed, and unlocked the door to admit his sister. Natalie held out the home phone, and he snatched it from her hand.

5

Bridgers

"Hello?...Oh, yes, pastor....Yes, sir, I'm ready." He smiled as he listened. "Yes, sir. I'll be there. And thank you."

Hanging up, Peyton tossed the phone back toward his sister, who ducked instead of trying to catch it.

"Nice." He grinned sarcastically and turned toward the closet. "Tell Mom I've got to leave early tonight. Pastor wants to talk to me before service. Did she get my gray jacket cleaned?"

"It's downstairs. And she said to tell you she's got dinner almost ready."

"And you couldn't bring it up? What's she making?"

"Mac and cheese."

Peyton turned with a scowl, and Natalie hurriedly clarified.

"The kind you like. Baked, with bread crumbs."

"No milk when I'm speaking, Nat! It messes with my voice. Tell her I'll have a hamburger if she can get it done in time. If not, I'll stop for something. Bring my jacket up and hang it on the door. I want to go over my notes one more time."

Natalie sighed and nodded. Peyton pulled a white shirt from the closet and kicked the door shut behind her. A few moments later, he stepped toward the mirror and surveyed himself carefully before raising his voice to yell, "Nat, where's my jacket?"

"It's hanging on your door," came the muffled response from Natalie's room.

Peyton slipped it on, looked himself over again, and straightened his tie slightly, then settled into a chair and reached for the freshly printed sheets sitting next to his Bible on the nightstand.

"Good evening, brothers and sisters. It's so humbling to be allowed to speak to you tonight and to share the message I believe the Lord's given me. I know I'm much younger than most of you, but I hope, like Paul said to Timothy, that you won't despise my youth, because we all know God's Word is greater than the messenger, amen?" A pause just long enough for the response, then, "That said, I'm still pretty new at this, so I won't complain if you do keep in mind how young I am—and forgive my mistakes accordingly." A slightly longer pause, and Peyton's apologetic smile widened into a satisfied grin. "The title of tonight's study—"

The water started to run in the bathroom sink, and he looked up to call, "You've got ten minutes before I have to fix my hair!"

Natalie's response was indistinct, and Peyton turned back to his notes.

"The title of tonight's study is 'God's Grace and Our Answer.' If you'll please turn with me…"

Chapter Three

Levi Allison grinned slightly as his father put down the phone and set the salad bowl on the table.

"So, Dad, is this a tossed salad or a layer cake?"

"Have at it." His father slid him the tongs and turned to his older son. "Asher, would you bless the food?"

"Sure, they always ask the seminary student," Asher complained with a grin, and his father punched him playfully in the ribs. When the blessing was over, Asher took the salad from his brother and studied his father critically. "Make any progress with the board?"

"Not much." Pastor Allison ran a hand through his barely-graying hair and shook his head. "You know, there is absolutely no church presence in that community—no congregation, no ministry, no outreach. We've got to find a way to get the gospel there—to show them that God loves them and so do His people."

"Sounds like you've got to convince His people first."

Pastor Allison sighed.

"That's why I'm hoping to get some of the kids interested. If they could start bridging those gaps at school, we might get an in-road that the board would be willing to follow up."

Levi glanced up with a frown.

"That's why you wanted to talk to Peyton?"

His father nodded. Levi dropped his gaze and began spearing tomatoes with his fork.

"I hear he has a lot of influence with the kids at church."

Levi nodded but didn't raise his head.

"So what's the problem?" Asher leaned forward and crossed his arms, and his brother swallowed hard and ran a finger along the edge of his watch.

"There was a—kind of a fight at school today. A couple of the guys messed with another kid's sneakers and got in trouble. They're friends with Peyton, and I guess he's—pretty mad about it."

"Sounds like your timing's impeccable, as always." Asher looked up with a rueful grin, but his father's eyes were fixed on Levi.

"And what do you think about it?"

"The other kid shouldn't have shoved them." Levi pushed a piece of lettuce around his plate, and his eyes flicked cautiously toward his father. "But they started it, and they were wrong."

"Did you say that?"

"No one asked me."

Pastor Allison sighed.

"Levi, I need your help with this. I know your school has serious problems, but we've got to start breaking down some of these walls, and you're in a better position to do that than anyone. You have to be part of the solution, not part of the problem."

Levi's face had lost its slight color, and his knuckles were white around his fork. His father laid a hand on his shoulder.

"Listen, son, I know talking to people isn't easy for you. But God's Spirit isn't a spirit of fear. You have to step out and trust Him with the consequences. I need you to be an example. Will you do that?"

Levi wet his lips, paused, then stammered, "I—I'll try."

"I was hoping for a little more than that." There was a definite ring of disappointment in his father's voice, and Levi's head drooped lower.

They finished eating in silence, and finally Pastor Allison glanced at the clock.

"I need to get going. I'll see you both at church."

"Dad?" Levi looked up, his face drawn and pale and his jaw clenched. "Can I come with you? I'll take some of the posters for the concert and hang them up near the bridge."

"If you can be ready in five minutes."

Levi bolted for the stairs, and Asher glanced up at his father.

"He's trying."

"He's avoiding." Pastor Allison shook his head sadly. "None of those kids is going to come out to a praise concert because of a flyer. And it takes a lot less courage to hang a piece of paper than to walk up and talk to someone."

Asher nodded slowly and pushed back his chair.

"If I come along, can I borrow some of your commentaries?"

"Sure."

After Asher had gone, Pastor Allison lingered in the kitchen for a moment, looking toward the stairs where Levi had disappeared. Finally, with a murmured "God, help my son," he turned and started for the door.

Chapter Four

"Man, my ma's gonna kill me when she finds out!"

Jamal threw a lumpy pillow across the room, almost knocking over the shadeless lamp in the corner.

"She'll kill you worse if you wreck the house." I didn't move from the spot on the floor I'd settled into when he'd started in two hours ago. Jamal slumped back into a chair and buried his head in his hands.

"What am I gonna do for two weeks, D? Sit around this dump? I'll go crazy!"

At least he knew I was in the room. That was improvement.

"Start with homework. All the chores your mama's gonna give you. Planning some way for us to replace your shoes."

"Us?" Jamal asked bitterly.

"Hey, man, you know I got no money, but I'm game to help out as long as you're not stealing. Picking up cans, washing cars, rapping at the bus stop—"

"D, you try to rap, and you're gonna owe money."

Jamal pointed a finger at me warningly, and his lips twitched in the first hint of a smile I'd seen all day. I glanced at the clock on the microwave and pushed myself to my feet.

"Your ma supposed to be home?" Jamal stood to follow me to the door, and I shook my head.

"Nah, but I plan to be good and gone before your mama gets back." I grinned, and he scowled. "Hey, man, you know you're lucky. She yells 'cause she wants better for you."

"If she kicks me out, can I crash at your place?"

No one in his right mind would want to crash at my place, and Jamal knew it, but I nodded.

"Sure. I got chores you can do, too."

Jamal punched me in the side, and I twisted his arm behind him before letting it go.

"Don't let it keep you down, man. You know I got your back. And I bet—"

"Don't say it!" Jamal groaned and put his hand up.

"What's that for?"

"That's to stop your everlasting 'I bet God still cares about you.' D, you don't even know what you're talking about, so how can you keep spouting that line?"

"Why not?"

"You heard what—two minutes—of some dude talking in the park when you were a kid? You don't know who he was, you never saw him again, and you never heard nothing like it since. But you still just act like it's true."

"I don't know, man. It feels right. Like if there's really a God out there, he'd be the kind that'd care about everybody."

"There's no way you can know that. I mean, what if his god was one of those weird statues with seven heads that you have to dance around and play creepy music and shave your head and all that? Would you still go for it?"

"One of those things couldn't care about anybody, forget everybody."

"So what if you found out he was from one of those bridger churches half the kids at school go to? You want any part of that God?"

I shook my head.

"This guy was different. If he was with them—well, somebody's got something wrong, that's all."

"Yeah, and maybe it was him. Like there is no God, or if there is, the only everybody he cares about are the people like him."

"Look, man, he was talking to old homeless Joe. If there's anybody who's nobody, it's gotta be him."

"All right, all right, forget it." Jamal threw up his hands. "Just don't expect me to change my life on the word of some random dude in the park."

I thought about his last words as I pulled on my jacket and headed down the stairs. I guessed what I'd overheard all those years ago had changed my life some. The words "God cares about you, me, and everyone" had been the last I'd heard before my mama called from the liquor store, but they had a way of coming back to me at the strangest times.

I'd known right off that a God who cared about everyone wouldn't like the way my mama treated me when she'd had a couple drinks, so when my friends started drinking, I stayed away. Same with drugs—I'd heard some pretty nasty stories about what could happen when people got high, and they didn't fit with that kind of God. And the whole point of a gang—sticking to some people so they could help you hurt others—it didn't take long for me to see the problem with that.

At first, my friends had called me "preacher," but I couldn't really preach with just that one line. After a while, they pretty much let it go as a part of me, even though they still grumbled when it got in their way. Maybe they figured a guy who thought that way wouldn't turn around and stab them in the back.

March had taken most of the edge off the cold, but the air was still chilly, and I stuck my hands deeper in my pockets as I paused at the corner.

My mama wouldn't be home yet, or if she was, she'd be gone again by the time I got there. I had homework that hadn't been done the whole time I sat at Jamal's, but something seemed to be pulling me over toward the bridge. I hadn't eaten, and maybe Anton at Luigi's would have some leftovers ready to throw out.

It was getting on toward dark, but Market and River streets were safe enough—or had been 'til a few months ago. Three fights and an attempted robbery—rumor was a couple of the gangs were looking to extend their reach.

I hoped they'd come to their senses. Killing the reputation of the only decent blocks on our side of the river would mean any of the good shops and restaurants would leave the neighborhood and not come back. Still, I had friends in both the Blades and the Scorpions, and they seemed content to leave me alone.

I zipped up my jacket and headed for Market Street.

Chapter Five

Levi shivered in spite of his heavy sweater as he reached the end of another block and glanced back along the river toward the bridge.

Dusk was beginning to fall, but not enough to be penetrated by the faint halos of the streetlights. Across the road, several businesses had already closed their doors, many doubly strengthened by tall metal gates. Around them, the neon signs of restaurants and bars blinked at intervals.

Levi looked at his watch and glanced over his shoulder, then ahead, then down at the stack of papers in his hand. He turned uncertainly, took a step, glanced at the papers again, and groaned.

Taking a deep breath, he ran his eyes over the patchwork of light and darkened windows on the other side of the street. He shifted as if to cross over, then hesitated again. The papers began to slip from his trembling grasp, and he knelt down to straighten them.

"This is ridiculous." The words were whispered through clenched teeth. "I'm not even talking to anyone. I've got to do this—something."

His teeth chattered as he stood up, and he clamped his jaw tightly in place. Whispering "God has not given us a spirit of fear" in the same strained undertone, Levi plunged across the street.

He passed a lamppost covered in lost dog notices and car-for-sale tear-offs, clenched his jaw harder, and turned back to add his own flyer to the mix. After struggling for a moment with the stack of papers and the unwieldy roll of tape, he finally managed to secure it on one end and stepped back to check its strength against the breeze. Shaking his head, he gripped the tape for another attempt.

Quick footsteps sounded behind him, and Levi whirled around, holding the flyers like a shield. Near the end of the block, a jogger paused at the corner of an alley. Levi groaned and leaned against the lamppost, gasping for breath.

"God has not given us a spirit of fear." The desperate whisper was barely audible.

From somewhere behind him, a dog barked, and Levi jumped. With a single glance at the still-flapping flyer, he started back toward the bridge at a trot.

Suddenly, loud shouts and cries erupted in the alley just ahead. Levi froze, then flattened himself against the wall.

For a moment, the air was filled with the sounds of scuffling feet, heavy blows, and ever-weakening cries, then something crashed to the ground. As Levi stood, still frozen, a rush of black-and-red-jacketed figures burst from the alley and across the street to the river, where they vanished into the night.

Levi stood trembling for a long moment after the runners had disappeared, then began slowly edging his way along the wall. Breathing heavily, he clenched his teeth and peered around the corner.

A single bulb was suspended near a padlocked service door, and within its circle of light, a figure lay on the ground, face down and arms outstretched, next to a pool of blood. Levi's eyes widened with horror. He took a step forward, staggered slightly, and clutched the wall for support.

Somewhere behind him, a door slammed. As though propelled by a starter's gun, Levi dropped the flyers and ran, narrowly missing being hit by an approaching car as he skidded across the street. His breakneck pace didn't slacken until he was safe within the walls of the church.

Chapter Six

"Construction, seriously? Why tonight?" Peyton's fingers drummed impatiently on the wheel, and Natalie sighed.

"It might have been faster to wait until they let us through."

"This way would be faster if we hadn't hit every single stoplight. I'm supposed to be early tonight."

"You can still make it." Natalie reached for the lock as she scanned the street outside the window, and Peyton gave a harsh laugh.

"What, you think they'll attack a moving car?"

"I just feel better with the door locked." His sister bit her lip and slumped back in her seat.

"Would I drive down here if I didn't think it was safe?"

"You wouldn't drive down here if they weren't working on Bly Street—Peyton!" Natalie threw both hands out to grip the dash as a running figure darted in front of them. Peyton jammed on the brakes and swerved, and the car lurched to a stop and died.

"Of all the—" Peyton slammed his hand against the steering wheel and winced in pain.

"What happened? Why'd it die?" Natalie gripped his arm, and her brother pulled away, still shaking his hand.

"I didn't get the clutch in when I floored the brake, that's all. That guy's just lucky I didn't hit this pole. I'd have had his hide."

"Dad's car never dies like that." Natalie managed a shaky breath.

"Dad's car isn't a classic." Peyton flexed his fingers with a frustrated groan and reached for the ignition. Suddenly, Natalie jumped backward and landed against his shoulder.

"Nat!" He shoved her back to her side of the seat, and Natalie turned a white face.

"Peyton, look!"

Her brother's eyes followed her trembling finger to a bloody figure lying halfway down the alley. For a second, they both stared in silence, then Peyton glanced at the clock, gave an angry exclamation, and started the engine.

"Shouldn't we do something?" Natalie's gaze stayed glued to the alley as Peyton nursed the clutch and put the car in gear.

"Like what, Nat? We're late as it is, and I've got to be there before service starts."

"He might still be alive. I think I saw his hand move."

"Let them handle their own problems."

"Peyton—"

"Natalie, I am late! You want me to leave you here?"

Natalie shook her head quickly as her brother pulled away from the curb.

"Should we at least call 911?"

"If you want to go back and give them whatever vitals he might have left, feel free. You can get out at the next light."

"Peyton!"

"Then let somebody else deal with it! We don't live down here, and if they want to beat each other up, it's not our problem. I've got a sermon to preach tonight, so if you want to do something about it, you go ahead, but you can count me out. Got it?"

Natalie threw one last glance toward the disappearing alley and sank back into her seat. Peyton checked the clock again and shifted into fourth gear.

Chapter Seven

I heard the sounds of the fight from a block away and slowed up, not wanting to get in the middle of a gang war or something just as bad. There was a thump like a body hitting the ground hard, then footsteps running in the other direction. That was strange—anyone wanting to get away fast should've headed for Market Street, unless the alley was blocked.

I waited a minute for the victors, if there were any, to come my way, but no one did. Another set of running footsteps, and a car screeched on River.

Whatever had happened, I knew it was not the sort of thing I wanted to be part of. Common sense said to get as far away as possible, but that sound of someone falling held me still. I thought of the younger kids that were sometimes used as messengers. If one of them had run into a rival gang, he might be in real trouble.

I waited a few more seconds to be sure no one was coming, then I hurried toward the alley.

What I saw stopped me in my tracks. The guy on the ground lay face down, not trying to get up. There was too much blood. It'd been more than a fistfight. A shooting? I hadn't heard a gun. A stabbing—that made more sense.

As I ran down the alley, I could see him more clearly. Dirty blond hair streaked with remnants of gel. A Woodbridge High athletic warm-up jacket. The kind of expensive running shoes I'd never even dared to dream about. I didn't know how he'd ended up here, but I didn't have to guess where he belonged.

Damp gravel dug into my knees as I dropped down by his side. Breathing. Check to see if he's breathing. I rolled him over as carefully as I could, and he moaned. Was that a good sign?

I put my ear next to his mouth and felt a tiny movement of air, so small that I wasn't sure 'til I'd felt it three more times. Blood trickled from the corner of his mouth—I could only hope he'd just bitten his tongue or knocked a tooth loose.

More blood streamed down his face from a nasty cut on his forehead, but that was nothing compared to the gash in his stomach. I'd seen a few knife wounds before—small ones, surface cuts, slices to an arm or leg, but this one was serious. The kid would bleed to death if he didn't get help. I'd never wished so bad for a cell phone—any phone.

Focus. I didn't have a phone, and wishing wasn't going to get me one. I'd have to do what I could 'til I could either move him or leave him long enough to get help. The bleeding had to be stopped. I ripped off my jacket and pressed it hard against the wound.

The kid groaned suddenly and moved like he was trying to sit up. I took one hand off the jacket and held his shoulder down hard.

"Don't move. Don't move!" I had to keep my voice calm, or I'd make things worse. I swallowed hard. "Just stay still, okay? Stay still."

Maybe he heard me, or maybe the pressure or pain was enough to keep him down. After a minute, I moved my other hand back to his stomach. He groaned again—it was an awful sound.

"Stay still. Don't move," I repeated. The blood had soaked through my jacket—I moved it and pressed it down again. If he could talk, maybe I could find out something that would help. Maybe he'd left his car somewhere or had friends waiting for him. "What's your name?" I asked.

No answer. I quickly checked his pockets for a phone or ID that might give me a clue, but nothing was there. Either a robbery had turned into a mugging or a mugging into a robbery. One without the other would've been more surprising. I leaned closer.

"Can you hear me? I want to help you."

A deep moan as his head moved a little on the street. He'd probably hit it when he fell, unless the guys who'd attacked him had done it. Several nasty bruises were already beginning to show under the blood on his face, and the rest of his body was probably just as bad. He'd be lucky if no bones were broken. I tried one last time.

"How'd you get down here? Did you drive?"

No answer. Either he was only half-conscious, or the pain was too bad to talk. Both made sense, but neither would help me find his friends. My jacket was soaked through again, and I moved it to a dry spot. Get the bleeding stopped, get him to a doctor.

I don't know how long I sat there folding and moving my jacket, then leaning over again to make sure he was still breathing, but finally the bleeding seemed to have slowed. I could only hope it wasn't because he was running out of blood.

I tied the jacket around him as tight as I could, hoping it would keep up the pressure, and tried to make up my mind what to do next. It was dangerous to move him, especially if he'd hit his head, but since I didn't know why he'd been attacked or by who or where they'd gone, I was afraid to leave him alone.

The next question was where to try to take him. I was looking for a car or a phone—I didn't care which. Some of the restaurants on River Street would still be open, but the way I looked, I wasn't sure if they'd even give me a chance to explain before they threw me out.

There was a garage four blocks over on 2nd that had a pay phone. It was a longer walk than I'd hoped for, but it seemed like the best plan at the moment.

In case he could hear me, I quickly explained what I was about to do, then as carefully as I could, I pulled his arms and head up over my shoulders, lifted him onto my back, and started down the alley. I'm a pretty strong kid, but four blocks suddenly seemed like forty miles.

Chapter Eight

Peyton threaded his way through the quickly filling foyer toward the hall that held the pastor's office with Natalie following like a nervous shadow. Pastor Allison stood near the door to the old choir loft talking with Mr. Fenton. Natalie started forward, but Peyton held her back.

"Never interrupt a deacon, Nat. Go find your friends. I have to talk to Pastor."

"There's not much time left. Can't I stay with you until Mom and Dad get here?" Natalie bit her lip and twisted the chain of her necklace around her finger.

"Fine, as long as you keep quiet."

Pastor Allison looked up and nodded, exchanged a few more words with the deacon, then came over to where they were standing.

"I'm sorry, Pastor. We ran into bad construction and had to take a longer way in. Do you still have time?" Peyton's tone was a model of apologetic deference. Pastor Allison smiled.

"That's all right. We can talk later. Sit in the front row, and I'll introduce you after worship. Then it's all yours. Nervous?"

Peyton shook his head, then offered a sheepish grin.

"Well, maybe a little."

"You'll do fine." Pastor Allison patted his shoulder, then turned to scan the crowd in the foyer. He frowned slightly.

"Did either of you happen to see Levi on your way in?"

"Levi? No, sir. Would you like us to look for him?" Peyton asked, and Natalie glanced up at him in surprise.

"No, that's all right. He was supposed to be walking back from across the bridge, and I haven't seen him yet."

"Across the bridge?" Natalie gripped her brother's arm, and he threw her a stern look.

"We drove in that way, and we didn't see him."

Natalie opened her lips, then closed them again tightly. Behind them, a door creaked, and Levi stepped out of the restroom, his flushed face freshly washed and his sweaty hair neatly combed. Natalie gave a sigh of relief and let go of Peyton's arm.

"All right, son?" his father asked.

Levi's eyes darted toward Peyton and Natalie, and he nodded.

"Good. I'll see you in service." With a squeeze of Levi's shoulder, Pastor Allison walked off, leaving the three teens together.

"Natalie." Levi awkwardly broke a few seconds' silence. "Peyton."

Peyton nodded, and Natalie smiled.

"You look like you were running."

Levi's face paled a little.

"I was—late." He pulled at his watchband, and his eyes fell to his shoes.

"So were we, only we had a car." Natalie grinned slightly, paused, then added, "I guess you know Peyton's doing the sermon tonight."

Levi nodded, and Natalie glanced up at her brother.

"Are you really nervous?"

Peyton scoffed.

"Seriously, Nat? They don't like you to be too confident. It sounds bad. I'm used to crowds." He scanned the foyer and nodded toward the back wall. "There. Mom and Dad just got here. I want to talk to some people before service."

He turned and disappeared into the sanctuary.

Chapter Nine

I could've sworn the blocks in my neighborhood had tripled in length. At this rate, we both might be dead by the time I reached 2nd. I leaned against a doorpost to try to catch my breath.

On the next street, someone pulled a chain through a lock. I took a hard gasp and dragged my aching legs toward the corner as fast as I could. This was too much for me. I needed someone's help—anyone's.

As I reached the cross street, I forced my head up in time to see someone leave the sidewalk in front of Taylor's Pawn and head for the opposite curb.

"Malik!"

At my yell, he turned, and his eyes widened when he saw me.

"D, what you doing here, man? What's going on? Who—"

"Malik, man, you gotta help me." I couldn't talk and hold on at the same time. I dropped to my knees and rolled my burden to the ground as carefully as I could. The bleeding had picked up again. I pressed my hands down hard on the jacket.

"Who is this? What's going on?" Malik started to back away, and I felt a wave of panic.

"Malik, please! He's cut bad, and I gotta get him to a hospital. Just let me use your phone."

"What's he cut with?" Malik took a cautious step forward.

"I don't know for sure. I found him in the alley."

Malik's eyes narrowed for a second, then flew wide.

"Stabbed?"

I had to nod.

"No way, man!" Malik started to back away again, not taking his eyes off the kid on the ground.

"Malik, he's gotta get help, or he's gonna die! Just let me call 911. You won't even have to pay."

"Man, they trace those calls! I don't want no cops crawling around my place 'cause somebody called about a stabbing."

I'd forgotten he didn't like to ask uncomfortable questions about the junk people pawned. I tried a different plan.

"Then just drive us to the hospital. Drive us and drop us off. Nobody has to know it's you. I won't tell, I swear."

"Take my truck over to the hospital for somebody to see and tell the cops? Don't tell me they won't be looking. Kid's a bridger, isn't he?"

"Yeah." I gritted my teeth. "But you know they won't be after you, man. Who stabs a guy and then takes him to the hospital?"

"Could happen."

"Yeah, and you could find a million dollars under the doormat. Don't give me that, Malik."

"What's he to you, man?"

"Nothing. But I'm not letting him die if I can help it."

"He's not going in my truck."

"Malik." As he turned away, I stood up, clenching my jaw like I was ready for a fight. "You help us, I won't say a word. You don't, I'll tell the cops you didn't."

Malik flinched hard and whirled around.

"You wouldn't."

"I would." I kept my eyes hard on his 'til he looked away. "Besides, I can't carry him any farther, so if he dies, it'll be on your doorstep. Think the cops won't ask questions about that?"

He shifted his feet nervously, and the key ring on his belt jingled. The sound took me back to the cluttered pawnshop with its overflowing storeroom. Suddenly, I had the answer.

"Do this, and I'll clean your place Sundays for a month."

"A month?" He was obviously hesitating.

"Two. And if I haven't done enough after that, you can tell me how much longer."

"And you don't give the cops no word about me?"

"Nothing, man, I swear."

After a second of silence, Malik muttered, "I'll get the truck."

I knelt down and checked again for the faint breathing.

"Hang on, kid." I still had no idea if he could hear me. "We're getting you help, okay? Just hang on."

Time moved in painfully slow motion as I sat in the back of the truck with the kid's head on my lap, trying to cushion the bumps and keep it as far as I could from the filthy sheet of plastic Malik had laid down to catch the blood. He wasn't breaking any speed limits to get us there—maybe not even hitting them.

The kid's face was whiter than I'd ever seen, and he'd stopped making any noise at all, even when I touched the gash. Looking at him felt like a knife through my own gut.

Now that I had time to think, all Malik's arguments and several of my own pelted me with accusations. What did I care? Who was he to me? Hadn't his kind tormented me and my friends? Hadn't I just left Jamal, who'd been punished much worse than he deserved while guys like this got off with a slap on the wrist? Why had I gotten involved in the first place?

Even as the questions came, I knew the answer. If God really cared about everyone, including me, then he cared about this kid, too. He could've been the meanest cuss in school, and maybe he was, but God cared about him, and that had to count for something.

The truck slowed down for a yellow light, and I groaned. Then suddenly a new idea hit me, and I looked up at the stars.

"I don't know who you are, or if you're really there." I'd never tried to talk to the God I'd heard about all those years ago, but just now it seemed like nothing could hurt. "If you care about this kid like I think, then can you do something, please? Just keep him alive 'til we get somewhere? That's all."

The light turned green, the truck turned a corner, and I looked up to see the welcoming lights of the hospital just ahead.

Chapter Ten

"That should do it for tonight." Asher locked the church door with the spare key and started down the steps to where Peyton and Natalie stood, nudging Levi with his knee on the way down. His brother jumped up and followed them around the corner to where Peyton's convertible was parked. "Not a bad set of wheels."

"It was my granddad's." Peyton's casual tone didn't mask his satisfied smile as he unlocked the car door. "He knew how much I liked it, so he left it to me when he died."

"That's quite a present." Asher climbed into the back and reached for the seatbelt, then nudged Levi and nodded toward his.

"Blessing and a curse," Natalie murmured as she slid into the front seat.

"Get off it, Nat. If they wanted it, they should've shown more interest. That's not my fault."

Natalie sighed, and Asher's eyebrows lifted slightly.

"People didn't like it?"

"We haven't talked to half our cousins since." Natalie bit her lips together, and Asher shook his head sympathetically.

"That's rough."

"Who cares?" Peyton's tone was defiant. "If they want to act like that, let them. Nothing I can do about it."

There was silence in the car for a long minute before Asher spoke again.

"Thanks for the ride. Sure beats walking."

"It's too bad your dad couldn't have stayed. I wanted to hear what he thought." Peyton frowned a little, and Asher laughed.

"Take my word. If you want to be a pastor someday, prepare for the life of the interrupted. It never stops, does it, Levi?"

Levi shook his head.

"Did he say what it was?" Natalie glanced up at the rearview mirror, and Asher shrugged.

"Just that he'd been called to the hospital. You can let your imagination run wild on that one, but speaking from experience, I wouldn't recommend it."

"And that's what you want to be?" Natalie turned a little in her seat.

"A pastor, or in the hospital?" Asher grinned, and Natalie giggled. "Yeah, a pastor, Lord willing. But if that's what God has planned, He's sure got a sense of humor."

"Why?"

"Because I dare you or anyone else to say 'Pastor Asher Allison' five times in a row without missing."

Natalie laughed again, and Peyton turned abruptly toward the back seat.

"So what'd you think, Levi?"

"Huh?" Levi jerked as if startled out of sleep, and Asher gave him a searching glance.

"The sermon. What'd you think?" Peyton repeated.

"Oh—yeah. It was good." Levi cupped his chin in his hands and stared at the floor. "I heard it last month at Sunday school."

"It wasn't exactly the same." Peyton's forehead puckered into the beginnings of a scowl. "I changed the illustration on the fourth point. Don't you think it worked better?"

"I—" Levi hesitated, and Natalie sighed.

"Peyton, not everyone memorizes your exact word choice the way you do."

"Which was the fourth point?" Asher shot another quick look at Levi, then directed his gaze toward the rearview mirror. "Thankfulness?"

"Growing a garden of gratitude."

"Right." Asher's eyebrow arched slightly, but he smiled. "What was the old illustration?"

As Peyton began to hold forth on the changes he had made and the logic behind them, his sister slumped back in her seat and stared out the window, and Levi closed his eyes and buried his face deeper in his hands.

Chapter Eleven

Once inside the hospital, everything was a glare of white lights, white uniforms, white sheets, and white floors. They had the kid on a stretcher almost before I could let go and rushed him back behind a set of official-looking doors.

Not knowing what to do, I stayed where I was 'til a doctor pulled me aside and asked me a couple questions about when it had happened and what I had done. Then he handed me off to a nurse, who gave me to a receptionist, who took me to a little room with a few flimsy tables and chairs, handed me a cup of coffee, and went to call the police.

I could've fallen down and kissed her shoes. Up 'til a few minutes before, I'd been too focused to notice the cold, but now that there was nothing left to do, I found myself shivering 'til my teeth chattered. I took long, slow sips of the coffee and tried not to think about the cops.

They must've been close by because they showed up before I'd finished the cup and while I was still shivering a little. Officer Joyce was a partly balding guy with a rock-hard scowl that would've taken a jackhammer to pry loose. Officer Sanchez was younger and thinner with a mouth that looked like it might smile if he wanted to let it.

I told them my story with no interruptions and was just starting to be glad it was over when Officer Joyce looked up from his notepad.

"You say you heard the fight, but you didn't see it."

I nodded, then remembered respect was a big thing with them. "Yes, sir."

"Where were you standing?"

"On Market Street, about a block down."

"And you didn't see anything?"

"No, sir."

"You didn't run over to see what was going on?"

"I didn't want to be part of it."

"But then you changed your mind."

"I heard someone fall, and I heard them run off. I thought somebody might need help."

"Regular Mother Teresa," Officer Joyce muttered sarcastically.

Officer Sanchez shot him a look, then turned to me.

"Was there anybody else in the alley when you got there?"

"No, sir."

"Did you notice anything they'd dropped? Anything they'd left behind?"

"No, sir."

"Recognize any of the voices? Or even just think they sounded familiar?"

"No, sir."

"Which way did they run off?" Officer Joyce growled suddenly.

"It sounded like they crossed River Street."

"And why would they do that?"

"I don't know, sir."

"Wouldn't they have been smarter to come back the other way?"

"Maybe."

"A lot less conspicuous."

"I guess."

"But instead, they ran off down River Street, in full view of all the bars."

"I don't know where they went. I heard them cross the street, that's all."

"Or maybe they did run your way." Officer Joyce snapped his notebook shut and leaned toward me without warning. "In fact, maybe you saw them, but you don't want to get them in trouble. Maybe they were even friends of yours."

"No."

"Members of your gang."

"No! I'm not in a gang, and I never saw them! They could've been my best friends or my worst enemies. Either way, I don't know!"

My hands started to shake, and I clenched them tighter around the coffee cup. Officer Sanchez took over the questions again.

"What about the boy who was stabbed? Any idea who he is?"

"No, sir." I tried to get my voice back to normal. I couldn't let them think I was nervous.

"Ever seen him before?"

"Not that I remember."

"Any idea why he was a target?"

"No, sir. Money, maybe. His pockets were empty."

"You went through his pockets?" That was Officer Joyce again with a tone that made me angry and scared all at once.

"I was looking for a phone to call an ambulance."

"You didn't find one?"

"Whatever he had, they must've taken it."

"So if we searched you right now, we'd find nothing?"

Suddenly, I felt hot all over, and I jumped to my feet.

"You'd find the key to my apartment and the rest of my lunch money for the week! Take it if you want! Search my place, too! Take my clothes for evidence—there's blood all over them, and it's all his, but you won't find a knife that's ever belonged to me anywhere in the city!"

By the time I finished, I was shaking hard, and for the first time, the sight of the blood on my hands and my shirt made me feel sick. Officer Sanchez put a hand on my shoulder and pushed me back into the chair with my head on my knees. After a minute, I was all right again, just more tired and shaky than I could ever remember.

"You had anything to eat tonight?"

I shook my head. Officer Sanchez pulled a candy bar from his pocket and handed it to me, and I ate it slowly. It helped some.

"Nobody's accusing you of anything, DaVonte." He threw a stern look at his partner. Maybe it was part of their act to get me to open up to him, but I didn't care. I didn't have anything to hide, and I was thankful for anyone even pretending to be on my side. "We just need to make sure we've got all the facts so we can try to find out who did this. Is there anything else you can tell us?"

I shook my head.

"What about the guy who drove you here?"

"He doesn't know anything. I found him a couple streets down and asked him for a ride."

"Someone you know?"

"I told him if he helped us, I wouldn't tell."

"If he's got nothing to hide, why would he care?" That was Officer Joyce again, and I lifted my head and looked him straight in the eyes.

"Because he didn't want you to think he had something to do with it—or knew more than he was telling—like you're doing with me. Everybody knows once the cops get their eye on you, they don't take it off. It gets you a name some of us don't want."

"So why'd you stick around?" Officer Sanchez asked gently, and I swallowed hard.

"I don't know for sure. I guess—I guess I want you to catch those guys. If not, a lot of people could get hurt—my friends, too. I'm sorry I can't give you any more."

Officer Joyce studied me skeptically, but Officer Sanchez got to his feet and gave me a hand up.

"Think you can show us the place where it happened?"

I nodded.

"All right. You take us there, and we'll give you a lift home."

Chapter Twelve

"Okay, kid, spill." Asher dropped the keys and his Bible on the counter and turned to face his brother. Levi jumped.

"What?"

"Don't give me 'what.' I saw you talking to Mrs. Farrell after service, then you disappeared for the rest of the night, and I found you in the sound booth editing worship lyrics."

"So?" Levi shrugged uneasily.

"So that's your church equivalent of shutting yourself in your room with a jigsaw puzzle."

"What's wrong with jigsaw puzzles?"

"Nothing. Except that they're your way of blocking out the world—at least the parts of it you don't want to deal with." Asher drummed his fingers on the counter for a minute, then sighed. "Come on, Levi, I know I'm not as good at this as Mom was, so you have to help me out. What did Mrs. Farrell say?"

Levi swallowed hard and turned away.

"You want me to talk to Dad instead?"

"Asher!"

"Then tell me."

Levi twisted his watchband slightly, then glanced up at his brother.

"She—she wanted to know when I'd be up there."

"Up there—in the pulpit?"

Levi nodded, and Asher sighed.

"Levi, we've been over this. If God calls you to something you're not naturally gifted for, then He'll give you what you need to do it. If He doesn't call you, then you don't have to feel bad about not being wired that way. Mrs. Farrell doesn't know you; she's just got a thing for pastors' sons following the family tradition—and you know how Dad feels about that."

Levi nodded slowly.

"Look, kid, unless you've got some new call from God that you haven't told us about, Dad is not going to be disappointed if you don't go into ministry, all right? Neither am I. And neither would Mom. Don't let some nice old lady who doesn't know what she's talking about throw you. You focus on what God's put in front of you."

"Got it." Levi's voice was low, and he shivered a little as he hung his sweater in the closet.

"Come on, snap out of it. Now I want your honest opinion on Peyton's sermon."

Levi grimaced slightly.

"Go ahead. Elaborate on that." Asher leaned against the counter and watched his brother closely, and Levi hesitated before he answered.

"He's a very good speaker."

"What about his points?"

"Huh?"

"Theologically sound?"

"Yeah—I mean, as far as I could tell."

"So what was the problem?"

"Nothing."

"There's something you didn't like, Levi. Is it the character underneath?"

"I don't know him that well."

"But you don't completely trust him. You don't relax around him."

"He—I don't know, Asher. I said I don't really know him."

"Impressions, then. What makes you nervous around him?"

"He just—he's—too careful. Like it's all part of a plan, or—like he knows all the right words that'll get him what he wants."

"A little overly polished for a kid your age?"

"I don't know. Maybe. And he's different with Natalie. Like he doesn't really care what she thinks, so he doesn't bother being nice to her."

"You think appearances might be deceiving? Like he's not entirely the great guy people think?"

Levi rubbed at his watch and turned away abruptly.

"Never mind. Forget Peyton." Asher straightened and reached for the cupboard door. "I'm going to make popcorn before I hit the books. Want some?"

Levi shook his head and started for the stairs. Asher sighed.

"Fine. Get some sleep and shake it off. I'll see you in the morning."

Chapter Thirteen

I shouldn't have been happy about the apartment fire on 10th Street, and I wasn't—not really. But I did breathe a big sigh of relief when I found it was the front-page story for the Graveside kids the next day at school.

Compared to that, a few cops showing up at an alley between Market and River was like a lost dog poster after a lion escape. All anyone wanted to know was if I'd seen the fire, and when they found out I hadn't, nothing else mattered.

I hadn't managed to get my homework done, but there was no fear of that getting around, since the one or two teachers that might comment on it wouldn't know 'til they sorted the papers after class. As far as I could tell, the only way I'd be caught was if the cops showed up for more questions like they'd said they might.

As I watched the bridgers in the hallways, I couldn't help wondering if any of them had noticed a missing face, even though I knew one day's absence wouldn't raise any eyebrows. The kid was an athlete of some sort—how long would it take for a name to trickle down into my circle?

I hoped he wasn't a football player—that would get instant coverage and way too much attention. A kid from the basketball team might get the kind of half-hearted interest I was hoping for—enough to spread the name but not pry into the details. Soccer—I'd never find out.

There was no real reason for me to learn the kid's name anyway. I just hoped the hospital had been able to find his family. Someone cared about this kid, and he'd need them with him.

By the beginning of sixth period, I'd pretty much put the whole thing out of my mind and was concentrating on some new type of equation when the intercom squawked from above the whiteboard.

"Miss Chan, please send DaVonte Jones to the office."

At the sound, Miss Chan jumped and dropped her marker—it was her first year teaching—but she gave a dramatic flourish with her hand the way she always did when something went wrong, and the class's snickers turned to applause. Her eyes met mine, and she nodded toward the hall pass on her desk. She was one of the few teachers who didn't have to check the roll to find me.

As I walked slowly toward the office, I tried to think of any other reason they might've called me. Something in my test scores the counselor wanted to talk about. I hadn't taken any tests. Somebody'd spray-painted my name on a wall. That'd bring the cops anyway. They'd found my mama somewhere. I took a deep breath and let it out fast. Questions from Officer Joyce sounded better all the time.

The office was deserted except for the secretaries and a janitor. I introduced myself to the lady at the closest desk, and she picked up her phone.

"Mr. Orbison, DaVonte Jones is here." She nodded and looked up at me. "Yes, sir, right away." Putting down the phone, she pointed a pencil at one of the doors. "The principal will see you in his office."

I'd spent my whole life trying to stay out of places like this. The door opened as I got close, and Principal Orbison looked me up and down.

"You're DaVonte Jones?"

I nodded, and he motioned me inside. After expecting—almost hoping—to see Officer Joyce and Officer Sanchez, the middle-aged couple sitting at the conference table was a shock. I tried to remind myself that detectives wore plain clothes and it wouldn't be surprising if the case had been handed off, but these two didn't seem like detectives. The lady had red, puffy eyes and looked like she'd forgotten her makeup. The man's suit was rumpled, and his tie was a little crooked.

The way they looked at me was hard to read—the fear and suspicion I'd grown to expect seemed to be mixed with confusion and something else I couldn't name.

"DaVonte." The principal sat down and nodded to me to do it, too. "Tell us where you were last night."

They probably wanted to catch me in a lie if my stories didn't match. I shrugged and went back over the details of how I'd heard but not seen the fight, found the kid in the alley, and gotten him to the hospital. The lady's mouth trembled a little while I was talking, and once I thought she wiped away tears.

When I finished, Mr. Orbison looked at the couple, and the man nodded.

"DaVonte." The principal cleared his throat. "This is Mr. and Mrs. Martens. Their son, Brett, attends school here. He's the boy you—found—last night."

I jerked my eyes back to the couple. No wonder they didn't know what to think of me! They'd probably never gotten within elbow distance of someone from my side of town—at least, not since high school—and now I was mixed up with their kid in a way they'd never dreamed.

"It was nothing," I said quickly. "I didn't know him—Brett—but I'd have done it for anybody."

"No." His mama dabbed at her eyes again, and her voice was shaky. "No, it was something. You saved my boy's life." She choked on the last word and buried her face in her hand.

"He's okay?" The question was out of my mouth before I thought. The kid was in the hospital with a knife wound, a banged-up head, and who knew what else. Of course he wasn't okay, but his dad seemed to know what I meant.

"He's all right. He'll be in the hospital for a little while, but the doctors said if you hadn't gotten him in when you did—" He swallowed hard and pulled nervously at his tie. "Well, he lost a lot of blood. He might not have—"

"I'm glad he's okay," I said quickly.

His mama lifted her head and dried her tears again, then looked into my eyes.

"He wants to see you."

"Me?" Now it was my turn to stare.

She nodded.

"We tried to tell him it could wait, but Brett can be very—"

"Stubborn," his dad put in as she finished with "determined."

"But—I can't—" I tried to protest, but I didn't know how. "They—well, they probably wouldn't let me."

"Yes, they would." His mama twisted the tissues in her hand as she went on slowly. "I know you have no reason in the world to do this, but it would be such a favor. For us. For Brett."

It finally started to sink in. She was actually begging me to come to the hospital and visit her kid. The more I thought about it, the more sense it made. If he'd gotten it in his head that he wanted to meet me, then he probably wouldn't rest right 'til he had. It wasn't something they thought they owed me—they were looking out for him. I nodded slowly.

"I'll come."

Chapter Fourteen

Levi finished loading his books into his backpack, then stood for a moment leaning his head against the locker. He had just picked up the bag and started toward the door when he was arrested by a voice behind him.

"Hey, Levi!"

He started and turned to see Peyton standing at the corner of a side hallway.

"You're coming, right?" Peyton eyed him with a frown, and Levi closed his eyes.

"I forgot it was Thursday."

"Listen, I need to talk to you."

"What for?" Levi gave a longing look over his shoulder but walked back toward Peyton.

"There's a couple kids from Wilson coming today. They're looking to start a Bible club and wanted to see how we do ours."

Levi nodded.

"So I thought you could start things out for us."

"Wait, what?" Levi took a step back.

"Not lead the meeting." Peyton rolled his eyes. "Just welcome them and introduce them to the group, then introduce me and hand things over."

"You can't do that?" Every trace of color had drained from Levi's face.

"What, introduce myself?"

"You always do—if there are new people."

"This is different."

"Why?" Levi put a hand against the nearest locker and leaned on it hard.

"Because they're guests."

"You said—we were showing them how we do things."

"That doesn't mean we can't make it special."

"You mean impress them." Beads of sweat gathered on Levi's forehead, and he wiped at them with a shaking hand. "You're president. I'm just part of the group."

"And your dad's a pastor. Isn't that part of the job description?"

"Hi, guys." Natalie's smile faded to a frown as she came closer. "Levi, are you okay? You don't look—"

"Peyton, I—" Levi swallowed hard and took a step backward. "I have to go."

"You're coming back, right?" Peyton's eyes narrowed as Levi shook his head.

"Sorry—I—" After a second's hesitation, Levi turned abruptly and rushed down the hall.

"Just great." Peyton crossed his arms with an angry sigh, and Natalie looked up.

"What happened?"

"I told the Wilson kids our pastor's son came to our Bible club, and now he bails at the last minute."

"Peyton, he looked sick. You can't blame him."

"Convenient."

"Don't say that."

"Fine. So how do you suggest explaining?"

Natalie shrugged.

"Just tell them the truth. Why wouldn't you?"

Peyton shot her a look of disgust.

"People miss all the time for all kinds of reasons. It's not a big deal." Natalie's forehead creased as her brother's eyes lighted suddenly. "What?"

"They were saying yesterday how pastors' families are always interrupted, right? I can just say Levi was supposed to open the meeting, mention that, and it'll all be good."

"Or you could just say he was sick and couldn't stay." Natalie bit her lip, and Peyton rolled his eyes.

"Do me a favor, will you, Nat?" His scowl deepened as he leaned toward his sister. "Just keep your mouth shut."

Chapter Fifteen

The hospital receptionist didn't even blink when I said I'd come to visit Brett Martens, and none of the nurses I passed in the halls paid any attention to me. I figured either his parents must've warned them I was coming, or else the hospital was way more used to people like me than I'd given them credit for.

I had no trouble finding the room, but once I got there, I stood outside checking and re-checking the number, raising my hand to knock, and then lowering it again. I had no idea what I was doing. What if the kid—Brett—was sleeping, and my knock woke him up? Was I supposed to just open the door? That couldn't be right. What if he'd changed his mind about wanting to see me? I found myself hoping a doctor or nurse would come by and throw me out.

After what seemed like forever, and just when I'd about decided to give it up, the door opened, and a nurse came out pushing a little cart. I took a step forward, then stopped, and she smiled like she'd seen it all before.

"You're here to see Brett?"

I nodded.

"You can go in. He's awake." She left the door open behind her and wheeled her cart into the next room.

It had to be now or never, and I'd promised his parents. I swallowed hard and stepped inside.

The room was like nothing I'd ever seen before, except maybe a science lab, but even with all the bandages and wires and tubes, I knew the kid on the bed right away. His eyes were closed, and his face was pale under the dark bruises, but at least it wasn't the same scary white as when I'd last seen it.

I stayed near the door for a minute, not sure what to say or if I should say anything at all. Then his eyes blinked open, and his head turned just a little. I knew when he saw me from the way his eyes suddenly went wide, and I stepped forward.

"Hey. They said you wanted me to come by. I can leave if you want."

About ten different expressions seemed to flicker across his face, but he finally said softly, "You found me."

I nodded.

"I heard you—I think. It's all a blur." He took a couple deep breaths and swallowed hard before he continued. "Dad said you were coming. I made him take Mom home—to get some sleep."

He tried to turn his head farther toward me but stopped and closed his eyes, and his face squeezed up in pain.

"Hey, take it easy." I sat down on a chair next to the bed where he wouldn't have to strain to see me. "You're still pretty banged up."

"Tell me about it." His voice was weak and shaky, and he didn't open his eyes for a few seconds. When he did, it was with a groan that didn't sound totally like pain. "I was so going to kill this season."

I smiled a little, remembering his jacket.

"What team?"

"Track."

I caught my laugh just in time. He might as well have been on the girls' badminton team as far as my hopes for getting a name through the school grapevine.

"I'm just glad you're alive," I said instead.

He didn't answer for a long minute, just laid there and looked at me, and the little I could see of his eyebrows under the bandage got closer and closer together.

"Why?" he asked finally, and I felt my own forehead wrinkle.

"Why what?"

"Why'd you help me? Why do you even care? What's it to you if I live or die?"

I'd been asked the question a lot in the last day, but somehow it sounded different coming from him. What kind of answer did he want to hear?

"I couldn't just leave you there."

His frown dug in further, and his head rolled back and forth just the tiniest bit.

"You didn't know me—but you knew who I was—how we treat you at school. Maybe I'm not the worst, but I'm sure not the best, and the—your friends—give it right back. Would they have stopped for me? Do you think I'd have stopped for you?"

"Maybe not." I shrugged.

"Then why?" He suddenly tried to sit up but fell back with a sharp groan, squeezing his eyes shut and pressing his arm to his stomach.

"Hey, hey!" I instinctively reached out to touch his shoulder, and as I did, my mind clouded with doubts again.

The kid was in the hospital now with plenty of people to take care of him. He could easily push the button to call the nurse, or I could. He didn't need me now like he'd needed me last night, and he'd just admitted what I'd already guessed he thought about people like me. Why had I come? Why was I still here? Why did I even care?

He groaned again, and his breath came in short gasps.

"Hey, man, it's okay. Take it easy. Just relax, all right?" I gripped his shoulder just a little tighter. Maybe sitting with a guy's head in your lap and begging a God you're not even sure exists not to let him die does something to you, because there was no way I could leave him now.

His breathing moved slowly back toward normal, and I finally felt the tension in his muscles slip. I let out a long breath and shook my head.

"You really need to learn to keep still, you know that? Keep that up, you'll rip something open, and the doctors'll have both our necks."

He opened his eyes for just a second, and I thought I saw tears in them before they closed again. I took my hand off his shoulder and laid it carefully on top of his hand.

"Look, if you want to know why—" I paused, searching for the right words. "I'm not sure, man. I can't really explain it—not very well. I just knew—well, if God cares about everyone, then that means people like you, not just people like me. That's all I was thinking, when I even had time to think. It was mostly just instinct."

He didn't say anything for a minute, then he asked without opening his eyes, "You know God?"

"Not really." I shrugged, forgetting he couldn't see me. "I heard someone say it once—that he cared about everybody—but that's about all I heard. I'm not even sure it's true—it just sounded right, you know?"

"God loves people like me, not just people like you." There was a strange tone in his voice, and I couldn't tell what he was thinking, but his hand shook a little, and I figured he'd probably talked more than enough.

"Hey, man, you better get some rest. I'll get out of here and let you sleep."

"No. Wait." He could hardly pry his eyes open, and his voice trembled with exhaustion, but I paused and waited for him to go on. "Do something for me, please? Two things."

His breathing was speeding up again, and I wasn't sure I should be letting him talk, but he rushed ahead like he was afraid to stop.

"Wait for my dad. He'll be back soon. Tell him—tell him I want to see the pastor."

My eyes opened wide.

"Are you okay? Should I get the nurse?"

"No." He squeezed his eyes shut. "It's not that. I just—I need to talk to him—that's all. Okay?"

"Sure. Okay. I'll tell him. What else?"

There was no answer for a few seconds, and I wondered if he'd fallen asleep, but just as I turned toward the door, I heard a faint whisper from behind me.

"Come back tomorrow."

Chapter Sixteen

"Natalie? Peyton? Is that you?"

"Yes, ma'am." Natalie closed the door behind her as her mother came into the hall, drying her hands on a kitchen towel.

"How was your club meeting?"

"Nothing special." Peyton started for the stairs, but his mother touched his arm.

"Peyton, before you start your homework, could you help me with an errand? Dad's working late tonight, and my car's still in the shop."

"What kind of errand?" Peyton's forehead creased slightly.

"I need to take a casserole to the Martens family. Lily's home now, but I'm not sure when she's going back to the hospital, and I'd like to get it to them tonight."

"Hospital? What happened?" Natalie's eyes opened wide, and her mother turned toward her.

"Oh, I thought you'd have heard it at school. Brett was hurt pretty badly last night—beaten up and stabbed, if I got the message right."

"Seriously?" Peyton's eyebrows shot up, and Natalie took a step back.

"Where?"

"I'm not sure. Anna Jackson thinks she heard it was down past the bridge, although what he'd have been doing there, I don't know. You two, please, never go down there alone. Ever. All right?"

Natalie shook her head hard. All the color had drained from her face.

"I don't know why you'd want to." Peyton glanced at his sister, and his eyes narrowed, but he continued speaking to his mother. "Sure, I'll take you. How long 'til you're ready?"

"Just about three minutes."

Their mother disappeared into the kitchen again, and Natalie lifted horror-stricken eyes to Peyton's face.

"You don't think—"

"No, I don't." Peyton cut her off decisively. "You think there was only one mugging in Graveside last night? That kind of thing happens all the time."

"But it could have been." Natalie blinked hard and bit her lip.

"If it was, how were we supposed to know? Brett had no business being down there, and we had no business stopping. Ten to one, if we had, it would've been some random deadbeat."

"What does it matter? Someone needed help—whoever it was—and it could've been Brett. We should've stopped—or at least called 911."

Peyton gave an exasperated sigh.

"Even if it was Brett—which it wasn't—he obviously got help without us. And who it might have been doesn't change the fact that I needed to get to church and you didn't want to be left there. End of story."

"But Peyton, what if it was?"

"I'm through talking about it." Peyton turned away, then suddenly spun on his heel to face his sister again. "No. I'm through after this. You make a big deal of it, you'll end up with the police involved. You want to go through all those questions and court stuff and who knows what else over something you didn't see and know nothing about?"

Natalie bit her lip harder.

"You have no idea what you saw the end of. Botched drug deal? Gang war? Murder? Sound like something you want to be mixed up in? You tell anyone, we'll both be in it, deep, and I don't want any part of it. I'd think long and hard about that if I were you. Tell Mom I'm waiting in the car."

Natalie sank down on the stairs and buried her head in her hands as the door closed behind her brother with a sharp click.

Chapter Seventeen

I couldn't tell if I felt more or less nervous as I walked through the hospital the next afternoon. At least I knew the nurses wouldn't throw me out, but I wasn't at all sure about Brett's parents. They'd asked me once, but they might not like the idea of my coming again, especially since my first visit hadn't done much to help him relax.

When I turned into the final hall, I noticed a man in a dark green jacket standing near the door, and as I came closer, he stepped out to meet me.

"You're here to see Brett?"

I nodded.

"You wouldn't happen to be DaVonte, would you?"

I nodded again.

"He's sleeping right now, but I wondered if I could talk to you for a few minutes while you wait."

I shrugged and followed him down a couple halls to a little corner with a few chairs and a table full of magazines, trying to decide if he was an off-duty doctor or one of the detectives I'd been waiting for.

"Brett was telling me about your conversation yesterday." The guy sat down in one of the chairs and nodded to me to take the one across from him. I was definitely leaning toward doctor and just hoped Brett hadn't really hurt himself talking to me. When I didn't answer, the guy went on. "He says you helped him because of

God—because you believe God loves him as much as He loves you."

I blinked, surprised that he'd gone into that kind of detail and not really sure how to answer.

"I'd like to find out what you know about this God."

This was definitely not what I'd expected. I swallowed and looked down.

"I don't know much, honest. I was listening to some guy in the park once when I was a kid. He was talking to an old bum, but I heard him say, 'God cares about you, me, and everyone.' I never found out any more than that—never knew for sure it was true, but it just sounded right. That's all."

"And that's the principle you've based your life on?"

I wasn't sure what that meant, so I kept quiet. He shook his head.

"You believed it was true, so you've tried to live like you believe it?"

"Yeah, I guess."

"Incredible." I'd never seen a smile quite like the one on the guy's face as he looked at me, but after a few seconds, it widened into a normal grin. "I suppose I should probably introduce myself. I'm Mark Allison, the pastor at West Arden. Do you know where that is?"

I'd forgotten all about the preacher Brett had wanted to talk to, and my mind scrambled to remember what I'd heard about them. Really good, or thought they were—kind of high up above everyone else—always talking about what you should and shouldn't do. The kind of guy that'd never be welcome in my neighborhood if he could ever lower himself enough to get there.

"The big stone building with the bell tower?"

"That's it. A very historic property." His eyebrows lifted in a way that made me grin in spite of myself. Whatever he thought of the building, at least it seemed like he wasn't a snob about it. "Ever been inside?"

I shook my head.

"The bus goes past it every day."

"You go to Woodbridge with Brett?"

"Yeah, but I never met him before. It's a big school."

"So I've heard. My son Levi's in the tenth grade there, but like you said, it's a big school."

I bit my lip to keep from laughing. A preacher's kid—that made so much sense! Levi Allison—there couldn't be two kids with that name—sat next to me in math class, and I'd worked with him on a couple group projects. From what I'd heard, preachers' kids were supposed to be as perfect as their dads—no wonder he looked like he thought tattoos were a contagious disease.

But maybe that was a little unfair. Sure, the kid stared—or tried not to stare—at my arms and my neck, but from what I'd seen, he had as hard a time talking to the other bridgers as he did to me, and the one time Miss Chan had called him up to the board, his hand shook so bad you couldn't read half the numbers. His dad was talking again, and I jerked my attention back.

"I had a long talk with Brett today. He's heard about God his whole life but never really done anything with it, never let it change the way he thinks or acts. Then you come along, not knowing half of what he does, but the part you do know, you act on in a very significant way. What you did for him was probably the best sermon Brett's ever heard. I can't begin to thank you, but I'd like to try to return the favor."

I had no idea what he meant, but I liked the way his eyes stayed fixed on mine. I couldn't see any fear in them, and he didn't look like he wanted to get away, the way most of my teachers did when I had to talk to them. Had everything I'd heard about preachers been wrong, or was this one totally different?

"DaVonte, I know the God you've been trying to follow, and I'd love to tell you more about Him—what He's done for you, and how you can know Him."

His voice was quiet, but the words hit me like a brick to the head. It was the moment I'd been waiting for ever since I was a kid, but now that it was here, I felt stunned and scared and helpless all at once. Jamal's question, "you want any part of that God?" flashed through my mind, and I wasn't sure how I'd keep going if the truth didn't match what I'd held on to all these years.

"Before I do that, though, there's one more thing I need to say." He reached out and put a hand on my shoulder, not even seeming to notice the tattoos. "DaVonte, what you heard that day was exactly right. God loves us—all of us—exactly the same, no matter our appearance, our background, or our bank account. Sometimes we forget that, and I know those of us in my part of town haven't acted that way toward those in yours. I'm sorry, and I'd like to change that. It won't be easy, but with your help, maybe we can start."

He wasn't making excuses or shrugging it off or acting like it didn't exist. I'd never seen that kind of honesty—not from someone like him.

I knew the problems in our city had started long before he was born, and besides, Levi'd transferred to Woodbridge from some small town in Idaho—or was it Iowa?—just before Thanksgiving. I was willing to bet his dad hadn't had anything at all to do with the bad blood between the two sides of the river, but somehow I liked it that he didn't point that out. I doubted he could really change anything, but at least he sounded serious about wanting to try.

It was the kind of thing the God I'd heard about would've been proud of. I swallowed hard.

"Would you tell me about your God? I think—I'd like to know more."

Chapter Eighteen

"So?" Asher gave his father an inquisitive smile as he took the dish of peas Levi held out.

"What?" Pastor Allison's forehead creased, and Asher shook his head.

"Are you going to tell us who got saved, or do we have to guess?"

His father set down his fork with a look of astonishment.

"How did you—"

Asher laughed.

"Come on, Dad, there's only one thing that makes you look like that. It is the reason you do what you do. Am I right, Levi?"

Levi darted a glance at his father's face and nodded.

"So?" Asher asked again, and Pastor Allison lifted his hands with a chuckle.

"I never knew I had a 'look,' but to answer your question, Brett Martens for one."

"Really?" Levi looked up from his plate with interest.

"Wake up call, huh?" Asher asked, and his father tilted his head slightly.

"Yes, but not the way you're thinking. It's quite a story."

"You said 'for one.' Is there another?"

"It's incredible." The far-away look came into Pastor Allison's eyes again, and he leaned back in his chair. "God works in amazing ways."

Asher shrugged at Levi and turned back to his plate, but their father's next question was directed to his younger son.

"Do you know a boy at school named DaVonte Jones? He lives in Graveside."

Levi silently mouthed the name, then his eyes widened.

"Does he have a huge eagle-flagpole tattoo most of the way down his left arm?"

"That's him." His father grinned, and Levi swallowed hard.

"He's in my math class."

"You can identify kids by their tattoos?" Asher laughed, and Levi dropped his gaze again.

"If you saw this one, you'd remember it, too."

"Well, it turns out he's the one who found Brett. This is where it gets amazing. When he was a child, he overheard what must have been someone witnessing in one of their parks. All he remembers about it is the idea that God cares about everyone, regardless of where they come from. And that, just that, moves him to action Wednesday night. That's what opened Brett's eyes more than anything."

"Wow." Asher shook his head as his father went on.

"I can't help thinking about that man in the park. You know, it's possible he went home completely discouraged, calling himself a failure. And eight, ten years later, his words are the key God uses to save Brett's life and two boys' souls. Don't ever, ever underestimate what God can do through a willing vessel, even if you never see the results."

"Wait, what happened to Brett?" Levi studied his father with a puzzled frown, and Asher's eyebrows shot up.

"Are you kidding? Where have you been the last two days? Or where'd you think Dad was? You seriously haven't heard about it?"

"About what?"

"Brett was attacked in Graveside on Wednesday." Pastor Allison turned back to his neglected plate. "He was out running; I guess the track coach had taken them down there before, but only as a group. I didn't realize it was dangerous that close to the river, or I'd never have let you go by yourself. Anyway, he was beaten and stabbed, a pretty close call. If DaVonte hadn't come when he did, Brett might not have made it."

"Do they have any clue to who did it yet?" Asher asked, and his father shook his head.

"DaVonte didn't see anything, and Brett says the whole night's a blur. Look at God's goodness, though, putting maybe the one boy in Graveside who'd be willing to stop and help a complete stranger from the other side of town right there at the scene."

Levi's chair scraped hard against the floor, and his father and brother glanced up. His face was white and strained, and he spoke through clenched teeth.

"Can I be excused, please?" His whole body trembled as he clutched the table for support.

His father nodded quickly, and Levi bolted for the stairs. Pastor Allison turned toward his older son.

"That came on fast."

"Maybe not." Asher pursed his lips as he studied the spot where his brother had disappeared. "He's been off the last couple days, but I haven't been able to pin it down."

"Physical or mental?"

"It's Levi. How can you tell if he doesn't talk?"

"When did it start?"

"Wednesday after church was the first I noticed. I thought I knew the problem, but now I'm not so sure."

"He seemed fine a few minutes ago."

"Until you told him about Brett." Asher's brow furrowed. "Just fear of what could've happened, maybe?"

"Wednesday night." Pastor Allison's eyes were vacant as he stared at the table. "The same evening Levi went down there with those flyers."

Asher's eyes widened.

"You don't think he saw something?"

"I don't know."

"Why would he hide something like that?"

His father shook his head.

"We're only guessing, and the timing could be coincidence. Either way, I'd better talk to him."

Chapter Nineteen

Brett's mama glanced up as I opened the door, but she didn't look scared or upset or even nervous like she'd been when I saw her at school. She even smiled a little. Brett turned his head slowly to follow her look and didn't close his eyes in pain the way he'd had to before.

"Hey." His voice sounded a little stronger.

"Hey."

"I thought you weren't coming."

"You were asleep when I got here, so you didn't think anything."

Brett grimaced, and his mama's lips twitched.

"You're going to get dinner now, right, Mom?" He didn't move his head to look back at her, and I couldn't tell if he just wanted her out of the room or if he figured this was his best shot to make her eat something. I could picture her as that kind—the mama that wouldn't take care of herself as long as she thought he needed her.

She put a hand on his and rubbed it gently as she stood up.

"And you're bringing me back a cheeseburger?"

"Whatever food he begs you for, don't give it to him." His mama raised her eyebrows warningly as her eyes met mine, and I nodded.

"Chocolate shake, then," Brett said, and she gently touched his hair.

"You're barely off clear liquids, and you already had a shake for dinner."

Brett groaned.

"I mean an actual milkshake, not chocolate-colored liquid cardboard."

I tried to bite my lip but couldn't quite stop the laugh.

"I think it's supposed to mean you're feeling better when you can complain about the food." I sat down in the chair across from where his mama had been and grinned at him, and Brett scowled.

"A dying donkey would complain about the junk they serve here. If this were prison, it'd be cruel and unusual punishment."

"So next time you want a change, try prison."

Brett tried to hold on to his frown, but the corners of his mouth were fighting to turn up.

"You want one of those alert bracelets that says, 'Don't save me—I hate hospital food'?"

The smile finally won out, and Brett snorted, then sucked in his breath and shut his eyes tight.

"Okay—better than the alternative. Barely." His words came through clenched teeth, and he groaned. "Don't make me laugh."

"Sorry." I winced and looked up at his mama, but she was still smiling. Maybe she was just glad he could still laugh, even if it hurt. She smoothed his hair again and left the room.

Neither of us said anything for a minute, but the silence didn't feel awkward like it had before. Finally, Brett opened his eyes and looked at me again.

"I'm glad you came."

I shrugged.

"What do your friends think about all this?"

"They don't know yet." I looked down and studied my hands.

"Will they be down on you when they find out?"

"I don't know. Maybe. Probably. They already think I'm half nuts."

"Would it be better if I didn't talk to you at school? I mean, when I get back?"

The question jerked my attention like the bus driver hitting the brakes hard. I hadn't even thought about the idea that he'd want to keep talking to me. Everything I'd done so far I could explain with basic human decency, but was I willing to risk the wrath of the whole school by crossing the line that'd stood for decades without a life-or-death reason?

I looked back up at Brett's bruised face and bandaged head, and other thoughts flooded my mind. The fear I'd felt when he'd almost died. The way I still wanted to look out for him, even if he didn't need me the same way. The prayer I'd prayed with Mr. Allison, asking God to forgive me for the things I'd done he didn't like.

This God—my God now, in a way I'd never known he could be—loved everyone, no matter who they were, whether they were in trouble or not. If I was going to love him like I said I would, could I tell Brett to keep away so the kids at school wouldn't hassle me? Truth should be worth living for. I swallowed hard.

"No. I mean, you don't have to talk to me, but you can if you want. Won't your friends be down on you, though?"

"I don't care." There was a strength in his voice that seemed to come from somewhere deep inside. "You saved my life, and I'm not forgetting that for some silly line someone drew across the bridge. Besides, if I'm going to be different, I might as well show it. Oh!" He lifted his head suddenly, then closed his eyes and fell back on the pillow, pressing his hand to the bandage.

"You okay?" I put my hand on his shoulder like I had before, only this time it didn't feel so strange.

Brett's face was white, and his breathing was fast and shallow. He didn't answer for a minute, and when he did, his eyes stayed closed.

"If I could just—stop getting dizzy—every time I raise my head." He took a deep breath and blew it out slowly between his lips.

"You hit it pretty hard, and it's been less than two days. Give it time."

"Yeah." Brett took another deep breath, and his shoulders relaxed a little. "Besides, if I get sick, I'm back to clear liquids, and I'm not doing that again."

I covered my mouth to hide my smile, then realized he couldn't see me anyway.

"What I was going to say—" His eyes opened, and he turned his head very slowly to face me. "Our pastor wanted to talk to you. He said he'd come back this afternoon."

"Already did." I grinned. "He talked to me while you were sleeping."

"Good." His breathing was faster again. "So—he answered your questions? About God?"

"Some of them."

Brett's eyebrows started to bend toward each other, and I shook my head.

"I just mean if his whole job is talking about God to the same people every week, there's probably a lot I don't know yet, right?"

"That's true." Brett closed his eyes again, and I laid a hand on his.

"But he told me enough. I mean, he told me about Jesus and how he died for me and what he wants from me. I never knew I could know God before, you know?"

"Do you?" Brett's voice was shaky, and I pressed his hand tighter.

"Yeah."

"Good." He was quiet for a long minute, then his eyes opened, just a little. "You know that makes us brothers."

"Huh?"

"When you believe in Jesus—you're part of God's family. That makes us brothers—with God as our dad."

I'd heard guys talk about their gangs like that, but this was different. With God in charge, the family would be all about love, not hate. I smiled.

"I like that."

"Sorry I can't come to church with you for a while."

"Forget it, man." Even if I had the nerve, I wouldn't be going to church for a while anyway—I still had a debt to work off for Malik. "You better get some rest, or your mama's gonna kick me out."

"Will you stay if I close my eyes?"

"If you close your eyes, you won't know."

He gave me a weak smile, and I shook my head.

"Fine. Get some rest. I'll stay."

Chapter Twenty

The unlatched door swung open at Pastor Allison's knock. Levi sat against the wall with his arms clutched tightly around his legs and his face buried in his knees.

"Are you sick, son?"

There was no answer at first, then Levi slowly shook his head. His father sat down next to him and put an arm around his shoulders. It was several long minutes before the silence was broken by a trembling whisper.

"I've got to be the worst Christian in history."

"Why?"

Levi swallowed hard and pulled his arms tighter around his knees.

"I—I was there, Dad. I saw—I didn't see it—I heard it—the fight. I saw guys running away—he was so still—there was so much blood—I didn't see his face—didn't know it was Brett." He drew a gasping breath. "I ran. I didn't stop to check—didn't stop to think, just—ran."

His whole body shook, and his father tightened his grip on his shoulder.

"I've been a Christian—since I was five. And a guy who—who doesn't even know God—only ever heard of Him once—acts more like one than I did."

The words ended in a sob, and Pastor Allison pulled his son's head to his chest, holding him close as he wept. After a minute, Levi pulled back, his voice cracking with raw pain.

"I can't do it, Dad. I've tried—over and over. I know—all the scriptures—but it doesn't help. I just can't beat it." He buried his face in his arms, and fresh tears streamed down his cheeks.

His father sat back and studied him for a long moment, then slowly shook his head.

"You know, son, I think you may have just found the answer." Pastor Allison closed his eyes and lifted his face to the ceiling for a brief moment before he continued. "Have you ever thought that maybe you're trying too hard?"

"What?" Levi's head jerked up, and his father smiled slightly.

"Why didn't you tell anyone what you'd seen?"

"I was—" Levi swallowed hard. "I was ashamed. Peyton and Natalie were there—and then it was too late—too late to help anything."

"You know you're not supposed to be afraid. So when the fear comes, shame and guilt and anger with yourself are always right on its heels, aren't they?"

Levi nodded slowly.

"In the first place, all of that takes your attention and energy away from the main battle. In the second place, what does it do for the way your body's always reacted to fear and stress?"

"Makes it worse?"

"That's not a question, it's a fact. If the shame and guilt can make you sick on their own—like tonight—then think what they're doing when you add them to your fear. If nothing else, they just prolong the torture. They keep eating away at you, pounding you for the battles you've lost when you should be looking ahead to the battles to be won."

Levi dropped his head to his knees again, and his father gently rubbed his shoulder.

"But that's only part of it, Levi. Here's where I think we've made our biggest mistake."

His son's head turned slightly.

"Yes, I said 'we.' I've never known fear as a crippling force, the way you feel it. I've assumed—and you've assumed—that if you just worked harder, strengthened your mind, applied more willpower, you'd be able to beat it. But I think you're right. You can't do it."

"You're saying—I should give up?" Levi closed his eyes again, and his tense muscles suddenly sagged.

"No. And yes." His father squeezed his shoulder harder. "What I'm not saying is to give up as a Christian, to decide you're no good and have no place in God's love. What I am saying is that this is a battle you can't fight. It's too big for you, like someone trapped in alcohol or drug addiction. There are some people that can work up the willpower to break through it on their own, but many, many others are just too weak. The chains are stronger than they are, and no matter how hard they try, they can't get out."

Levi shuddered, and his father pulled him close again.

"Son, I'm not saying that to discourage you. You've heard stories all your life about people who were trapped in those things. What got them out?"

"God." The word was a whisper.

"And God wants to deliver you from this bondage to fear. You can't do it, no matter how hard you try, but He is stronger. Stronger than addiction, stronger than fear, stronger than any chain the enemy can use to bind us."

"I know—"

"Yes, you know, but you're going about it the wrong way. You're trying to break the chains yourself with what you know and what you think you should be able to do. You need to stop trying. Stop letting the battle rise and fall on your strength or weakness. Let God do this for you, Levi. Go to Him and admit that you can't win this fight. It's got to be His Spirit or nothing. Ask Him to do this work in you. Do you believe He can?"

"Yes, but—I have to do something—don't I?"

"You have to let His Spirit work. Trust Him enough to step out and do what He puts in front of you, and trust that He'll carry you through it. Don't try to work up the courage to face it. That's where you fail. Step out, even when you're shaking in your shoes, and trust God to give you what you need in that moment."

Levi shook his head slowly.

"It just sounds like—like a cop-out. Like I'm asking God to do something I should be able to do myself."

"That's pride, son. A very disguised and a very deadly form. You can try all your life to be the person God wants you to be—working in your own strength and trusting Him for salvation and no more. Or you can go to Him and admit that you can't hit the mark—not just for salvation but for your daily struggles. You can fall on your knees and ask Him to do what you can't and learn to say with Paul, 'When I am weak, then I am strong.' It's your choice, Levi. But God's waiting for you. He can do more in you and through you than you could ever dream—if you'll just stop trying and come."

Chapter Twenty-One

I'd never felt so glad for the weekend, but between all the homework I'd missed and a whole day working at Taylor's Pawn, it seemed like it had barely started when Monday morning and the bus rolled around.

For once, I was glad Brett was still in the hospital. I hadn't had any time to think about what I'd say to my friends after the word got around, and I sure didn't mind putting it off a little longer.

The apartment fire was old news, but the cops hadn't made a big enough stink about the stabbing to draw much interest, and my vague excuses seemed to satisfy the few guys who'd noticed I hadn't been around. Malik had just about worked me off my feet, and I decided to put everything about the last few days out of my mind, at least 'til I wasn't too tired to think straight.

When lunchtime came, my class was one of the first in line, and I took a seat at a back table and closed my eyes, wondering if I could manage to catch a few minutes' sleep in all the chaos. Probably not with the undefinable smell of today's "meatloaf special" in front of me. What had they put in that, anyway? I guessed it was better not to know, but at least I'd been safe and gotten extra ketchup. I opened my eyes and reached for my fork.

"Hey." The voice off to the side was just a whisper, but my head spun around. Levi, one of the bridgers from my math class, stood next to the table beside me, but his eyes were turned in my direction. I squinted at him, not sure if he'd even meant to talk out loud.

"I just—I, um—" The kid's knuckles were white on his tray, and his eyes blinked like they couldn't find the off switch. "You—you're in my—my math class, right?"

I nodded, wondering if we all really did look alike to them, or if he was just reaching for something to say. He swallowed hard.

"I—I wanted to say—I wanted to tell you, I—I—" He rocked backward just a little and almost fell over the bench behind him.

"Look, you want to sit down before you fall down?" It was not a good idea, and I knew it, but the kid was as white as a blank sheet of paper, and concern was eating away at the edges of my common sense.

He dropped onto the bench in front of me with a sigh, but his eyes stayed locked on mine like he was afraid he'd lose his nerve if he looked away.

"I—I'm sorry."

"For what?"

The shock of the words cleared my brain a little, and some of the pieces started falling into place. Levi Allison—the kid of the preacher I'd met at the hospital. Had his dad told him to talk to me? That would explain a lot, but I still couldn't think of anything he'd done that deserved an apology.

"For not—for letting you think—" He swallowed hard and took a couple deep breaths, and his eyes closed for just a second. When he opened them again, his words rushed out like rain from a clogged gutter.

"I don't look down on you for where you come from—or anything like that—but I let you think I did—or I never said anything to tell you I didn't. I let you think I was like the other kids who—who didn't want anything to do with you. I'm a Christian, and I—I don't think that way. I'm sorry I didn't act like it."

The kid's hands were shaking by the time he finished, and he gulped air like he'd just run five blocks. The corner of my mouth started to turn up, and I shook my head.

"Didn't act like it how? By not coming over to talk to me? How many bri—kids from Woodbridge—have you just randomly started conversations with?"

His eyes flicked up, then down again.

"Not many."

"That's what I thought. So you weren't treating me—us—any different, right?"

"No. Maybe. But I—I could've said something—when the other kids were talking bad about you."

I wasn't sure if the "you" was me specifically or the Graveside kids as a whole, but the idea was so funny I couldn't hold back a laugh.

"What?" Levi looked up.

"No offense, but seriously?"

His face was a living question mark, and I shook my head with a grin.

"I mean, come on. You're probably the kid who threw up the first time you had to talk in front of the class, right?"

A tiny, thin smile flickered on his lips.

"The first time?"

"Okay, every time." I laughed again. "And you're supposed to suddenly go all Joan of Arc on all your friends and a bunch of kids you don't know because they're making cracks about a bunch of other kids you don't know?" Joan of Arc—that was a great pick. Just what every guy wanted to be. I shook my head. "Sorry, I'm up to my eyeballs in France right now."

"Yeah, me, too." Levi's mouth curved into an actual grin. "It is a pretty funny picture. But—" He swallowed hard, and his face turned serious again. "But I am going to try—not Joan of Arc, but— some things are worth standing up for—even if I'm not the best person to do it. Besides—"

"Hey, you! What, are you lost?"

We both jumped at the sudden challenge, and my heart sank as I looked up. Tyrell "T-Rex" Harrison had come up beside me and was glaring at Levi—I must've been really tired not to notice him.

Levi shook his head quickly. His face had gone white again, and this time with good reason.

"Well, you better get lost! And fast! What, taking the good seats isn't good enough for you? You gotta take ours, too, just 'cause you can?" Tyrell gave Levi a shove that almost knocked him off the bench.

"Tyrell, leave him alone. He's not bothering anybody." I wasn't ready for this. How was I supposed to explain? Who would ever listen to me now, with T-Rex on the other side?

"Yeah, well, he's bothering me. You little rich kids make me sick. Trying to act like you own the world. Well, here's one place where your money's no good."

His eyes flicked toward Nick Russo, who'd come up behind Levi, but there was no time for a warning. Another shove and a yank on his backpack, and Levi fell hard to the floor, knocking his head against the next bench. I jumped up just as Tyrell swept his tray off the table, splattering Levi and the floor with milk, ketchup, and oily meatloaf.

"I said leave him alone!"

Tyrell turned to face me, looking half angry and half smug.

"Oh, yeah, man, what's he to you? Your new best friend? I always knew you weren't one of us."

That taunt usually made me fall back on the reasons I was and they knew it, but somehow this time it didn't sting like usual.

"Yeah, well, maybe I don't want to be. Not one that bullies kids 'cause they're different from me. Not one that slaps people in the face 'cause they try to act decent for once. Not one that tells my friends who they can and can't talk to. I thought this was a free country."

I knew every eye within hearing distance was on me, but I kept my focus on Tyrell as I moved slowly to the other side of the table.

"You know, we slam them for keeping us out—judging us by our clothes—thinking they're too good for us. But we're doing the same thing. Or we were. I'm not—not anymore. From now on, I'll talk to whoever I want. And whoever wants to talk to me, anybody that messes with them messes with me. I'm Graveside all through—you all know that. But I'm something else now, too. Anybody who wants to know more, just come and talk—if you have the guts."

Levi was sitting up now, leaning on his knees with his hand on the back of his head. I took hold of his elbow and helped him up, brushing off the meatloaf as he stood. He leaned against me but didn't make a sound as we left the cafeteria.

Chapter Twenty-Two

Levi closed his eyes and leaned his head back against the wall as DaVonte worked at the splotches on his shirt with wet paper towels.

"Forget it. It's nothing."

"You want to bleed ketchup all over the place? I mean, I'm not saying it won't stain, but you look like a human french fry."

"I knew yellow was a bad choice." The corner of Levi's lips turned up, and DaVonte laughed. "By the end of the day, I'm going to smell like a milk-drenched meatloaf, so it doesn't much matter."

"The end of the day?"

"Right. I smell like one now. By the end of the day, I'll smell like rotten meatloaf drenched in sour milk. Thanks for reminding me." Levi rolled his neck back and winced, and DaVonte frowned.

"How's your head?"

"It'll be okay. I saw stars for a minute, but it's better now."

"You should probably go to the nurse."

"So she can tell me I have a lump on the back of my head? I've already figured that out, thanks."

DaVonte laughed again and punched him gently on the knee.

"You got a real sense of humor when you start talking. Or maybe it's the bump on the head. I mean so she can give you a painkiller and maybe some ice to put on it."

"Right. The sense of humor's my brother's. You were really great in there."

"Like Joan of Arc?" DaVonte grinned, and Levi laughed.

"Right. Like Joan of Arc. Where do you suppose she ate lunch?"

"Before or after they burned her at the stake?"

"Either. More to the point, where are we supposed to eat from now on?"

"I'm guessing your side's out of the question."

Levi sighed.

"They might not knock you off the bench—I can't guarantee it—but they'll definitely find ways to show you're not welcome. Why does the line have to be down the middle of the cafeteria? There's no in-between tables."

DaVonte frowned slightly.

"No, but there is an unused one."

"You mean the one by the lunch line where you can't hear yourself think?"

"Only empty table I know of."

"So how much do we want this?" There was an honest question in Levi's eyes as he looked up, and DaVonte's forehead creased.

"What exactly is it that we want?"

"To show the world—at least, the school—that we care more about what God thinks than other people—I mean, what other people think. We both know how we feel, but what difference does it make if we don't show it?"

"You really think we're up to this?"

"Just like Joan of Arc." Levi grinned weakly.

"You know, we just might get burned at the stake."

"So is it worth it?"

DaVonte looked down at his shoes for a minute, then he raised his head to meet Levi's eyes.

"I'll do it on one condition."

"What's that?"

"You bring the earplugs."

"Deal." Levi grinned and held out his hand. DaVonte shook it, then cocked his head thoughtfully.

"You know, Brett might join us if he gets the chance. I don't know what period he has lunch. If the noise doesn't do a number on his head."

"Oh!" Levi sat forward, sucked in his breath, and grasped the back of his neck. DaVonte rolled his eyes.

"You two are so much alike. Would you stop trying to kill yourself by moving too fast?"

"That's the other thing I was going to tell you when we were—interrupted."

"Attacked?"

"Blindsided. Don't get me started. But about Brett—I wanted to thank you. And to apologize."

"For Brett?" DaVonte's forehead creased.

"For not helping. For leaving it to you." Levi swallowed hard. "I was there that night—on River Street. I heard the fight—saw a bunch of guys running away—saw him lying there all bloody, and—I ran." His shoulders slumped, and he didn't meet DaVonte's eyes.

"That's enough to scare anybody." There was no contempt in DaVonte's tone, but his eyes widened suddenly. "You said you saw the guys running away?"

"Not their faces, just their jackets. I told my dad on Friday, and he took me to the police station. They got this look on their faces like they knew something, but they didn't tell us what it was."

"What were their jackets?" DaVonte leaned forward eagerly.

"Black and red—red on the hoods and sleeves."

DaVonte sat back with a long, slow whistle.

"You know who they were?"

"Black Widows. No wonder they ran off toward the river! They're not from Graveside—they're way east of us. I'd heard the gangs were trying to move in on River Street, but I never knew the Black Widows were part of it. Sooner the cops put a stop to that, the better. They're deadly."

"I should've said something sooner." Levi dropped his head again, and DaVonte shrugged.

"Maybe. But this might work out better anyway. If no cops came looking right away and they thought nobody saw them, they probably got careless. Maybe even held on to the knife. There were some bloody footprints in the alley—if the cops can find those sneakers, they're done." DaVonte let out a long breath and grinned. "That should get me off the hook anyway. Thanks for telling me."

"They thought you were in on it?" Levi glanced up, his eyes wide with concern.

"They thought maybe I was protecting the guys that were."

"I should've said something sooner." Levi winced and looked away again, rubbing the back of his neck.

"Over. Lesson learned. No hard feelings." DaVonte stood and held a hand out. "Come on, let's get that lump looked at. Sorry about your lunch."

"I'm not that hungry anyway." Levi sighed as he let himself be pulled up. "What about yours?"

"I'll live. Even thank you if everyone else gets food poisoning from that meatloaf. You ought to have the nurse take a sample of it for lab tests."

Levi attempted a grin.

"Right now, I'll settle for some ice. But since I cost you lunch, would you come over for dinner sometime? I mean, to my house? My brother would love you, and I know my dad wants to see you again."

"You think that's going too fast?"

"To change the world? We've got to start somewhere. Might as well be hung for a sheep as a lamb."

"What?" DaVonte stared at him, and Levi grinned as he closed his eyes and rolled his neck back.

"It's something my grandma used to say. If they're going to burn us at the stake anyway, we might as well do enough to earn it."

"Go big or go home."

"Exactly." Levi met his gaze, and DaVonte laughed.

"Okay, Joan. Lead me to the Arc."

Chapter Twenty-Three

Before I left Levi in the nurse's office, we'd settled on Tuesday, as long as our parents okayed it. I let that stand, knowing my mama wouldn't care but doubting I'd see her long enough to ask. I'd pushed for the extra day, not at all sure the nurse wouldn't send him home or for x-rays and because I'd promised to visit Brett again after the weekend.

True to my prediction, Levi didn't show up in math class that afternoon, but the next day as I hesitated in the cafeteria, he came up behind me.

"We still doing this?"

"I wasn't sure you were here."

"Takes more than a knock on the head to keep me down." Levi grinned, but I could tell he still had a headache.

"You want another day to let it settle before braving the madness?"

"Where, exactly?"

"I mean by yourself. At your own table."

Levi shook his head.

"This is my table. I picked it, and I'm sticking with it. You don't have to come."

I guessed I deserved that. I shook my head.

"You bring the earplugs?"

Levi's grin widened, and he dropped a small plastic bag onto my tray.

"Then I'm coming."

"Brought more in case anyone else wants to join us."

We practically had to yell to be heard as we settled ourselves at the one unclaimed table. I rolled my eyes.

"You're not hopeful—you're nuts."

"That's what they said about Joan of Arc." Levi laughed, and it sounded good. "Did your mom okay tonight?"

"I didn't see her. Left her a note. She didn't answer." I swallowed hard. "She never cares where I go, but I don't know if your dad's okay with that. If he wants full-on permission, it could be a while."

"We'll ask." Levi looked unsure, and I figured none of his other friends would get away with leaving it there. Problem was, I wasn't trying to hide things from my mama—I'd have told her everywhere I went and everything I did, if she'd ever wanted to know.

Levi closed his eyes and bent his head over his hands for a minute, then looked up again and reached for his tray.

"You okay?" I asked, and he laughed.

"Just blessing my food. I forgot you're new to the whole Christian thing."

"Your dad didn't tell me about that."

"It's not a requirement." Levi grinned. "But Jesus did it, so we do it, too."

"What are you doing?"

"Thanking God for the food—even if it is fish sticks—and asking Him to use it to nourish our bodies and keep us strong for His work—even if it is fish sticks."

"Are there special words?"

Levi shook his head.

"Just talk to Him from your heart. That's what's important."

I bent my head over my hands the way he'd done. Pray from my heart—it was what his dad had said, too.

I thanked God again for what he'd done for me, and for Levi and Brett, and I prayed that he'd show me how to talk to the kids in my neighborhood about him. I prayed that I'd learn to follow him better and that my mama could someday know him, too. I'd almost forgotten about the food, but I remembered just as I was finishing and thanked him for it—even if it was fish sticks.

When I opened my eyes again, I saw Reese Mason and LaShawn Barker watching me from the lunch line. This would be all over the Graveside section in five minutes. I let out my breath slowly and turned back to Levi.

"You all right?" He looked concerned, and I smiled.

"I'm new at this praying thing. I probably put way too much in."

"The more the better—most of the time. Maybe not if other people are waiting on you." Levi grinned, but his eyes still looked worried. "I didn't mean that. You've got more at stake here than I do—at least, more friends to lose. Are you sure you're up for this?"

He'd seen the looks, too, and understood a little of what they meant. I bit my lips together.

"You want to go back?"

He shook his head.

"I never said that. But I won't blame you if you do. It doesn't have to mean going back to not being friends."

The thought tempted me for about five seconds, then I shook my head.

"Just going back to not being allowed to act like it or tell anyone or talk to you when we're not alone. No. I'm in this thing, and I'm not backing down."

If I'd needed a reward, Levi's smile would've been enough. He picked up a fish stick and held it out in front of him.

"Joan of Arc?"

"Joan of Arc." I laughed and crossed swords with one of my own fish sticks.

"And better examples than that." Levi dipped his sword in ketchup and crunched it with a grin. "Jesus went all kinds of unpopular places and did all kinds of unpopular things—talked to all kinds of unpopular people, too."

"That'll be us, if it isn't already." I glanced at the rest of the table, still sitting empty, and a new thought hit me suddenly. "You think if he was here, he'd sit at this table?"

Levi nodded.

"I think He would, and He is. And I'm glad I am, too—even if it took me too long to get here."

"You're here now, and so am I. I just don't know where the others are supposed to come from."

"We'll pray."

A pan dropped in the kitchen with a bang, and Levi closed his eyes and sucked in his breath. I shook my head. Even Joan of Arc might not have been nutty enough to brave this racket with a bad headache, but maybe Jesus would, for a good enough reason. Levi opened his eyes slowly and blinked them hard.

"All right?" I asked, and he gave me a weak grin.

"Perfect. I'm due for more painkillers after lunch anyway."

"What'd they do with you yesterday?"

"I wanted to go back to class, but the headache kept getting worse, so they called Asher—my brother. He's in seminary—online, so he's home most of the day. Of course, he and Dad wanted me to get checked out at the hospital." He sighed.

"And what'd they say?" I knew I didn't have to ask if he'd gone.

"No breaks, no brain damage. I'll have a headache for a while, and I should keep my hands off the bump. I could've told them that."

"What, are you a medical student?"

"Now you sound like Asher. Maybe I shouldn't let the two of you meet."

I shrugged, and he grimaced.

"I'm kidding. You don't get off that easy. He's picking us up today. Be on the west stairs after class. I'll wait for you."

"And if I need my mama's permission?"

"Then we'll take you home. If you're nice to Asher. If not, he'll make you walk."

Chapter Twenty-Four

"Glad you both made it." Asher grinned as Levi opened the car door and slid into the back seat with DaVonte.

"Me, too, but we have a permission question." Levi glanced at DaVonte, who sighed.

"I left a note for my mama, but she didn't answer it, and I didn't see her last night. She never cares where I go, but if I need special permission, I can't stay."

Asher's eyes showed sympathy, and he nodded.

"We'll ask Dad when he gets in, but I don't think it's a problem. If he disagrees, we'll just take you home."

"Good." Levi relaxed against the seat, and Asher glanced back at him.

"How's the head?"

"Better."

"Even after lunch?" DaVonte eyed him skeptically, and Asher's eyes narrowed.

"What happened at lunch?"

Levi grinned.

"We started our grand experiment—the table no one else wants. I told you about it."

"Right. I forgot. How did it go?"

"We lasted the whole period. No one else joined us. Half the school gave us strange or dirty looks the rest of the day, and the other half will have them by tomorrow."

"You're awfully cheerful about that."

"It feels good." Levi's smile didn't waver. "Not the dirty looks, but knowing we're doing what God wants. It's worth it."

"I'm proud of you, Levi." Asher's voice was soft, and his brother blinked hard and turned to look out the window. Asher glanced back in the rearview mirror. "And you must be DaVonte. I guess I didn't really give Levi a chance for an introduction. He couldn't stop talking about you last night. Thanks for looking out for him."

"I didn't do much." DaVonte looked down, and Asher shook his head.

"Didn't see it coming, maybe, but you stood up for him and did what you could. I really appreciate it."

"Speaking of introductions." Levi turned back from the window. "DaVonte, this is my brother, Asher."

"Didn't I say that?" Asher laughed, and Levi shook his head with a grin. "Okay, then I'm as bad as you are. You guys want ice cream on the way? It's early enough."

"Early enough for what?" DaVonte's forehead wrinkled, and Levi laughed.

"Not to spoil dinner. Asher's cooking. Take the ice cream."

"All right, smart alec. You don't like it, you can make your own. DaVonte, what do you say? I'm buying."

"Then I guess I'm in." DaVonte shrugged and looked at Levi.

"Told you he was smart." Levi grinned, and Asher laughed.

"Ice cream it is. And when we get home, you both hit your books for at least an hour. Deal?"

"While you start dinner?" Levi's eyes twinkled. "Sounds good, as long as you leave time to call the pizza place, just in case."

"Watch it, kid, or I'll spit on your plate. And if this is what you're going to be like hanging around DaVonte—"

"What?" Levi threw an uneasy glance at DaVonte, who bit his lips together and looked away.

"Then I'm asking him to keep it up, whatever it is. I haven't seen you this way in a long time. I've missed it."

"Don't do that!" Levi thumped his brother's seat and rolled his eyes at DaVonte, who gave a shaky laugh. "I told you I wasn't sure you should meet him."

"I thought you said you weren't sure he should meet me."

"Well, I stand by both. You're never allowed to be together without me, or I'm doomed."

DaVonte grinned, and Asher raised his eyebrows mischievously.

"Sounds like a challenge to me. What do you think, DaVonte?"

DaVonte glanced back and forth between them, and finally his grin widened.

"I guess if I have to choose, I'll stick with Levi. I did just probably lose all the rest of my friends for him—it wouldn't be very smart to throw him off now."

"Fish sticks?" Levi tipped his fist toward his friend.

"Fish sticks." DaVonte returned the salute. "And Joan of Arc."

Both boys laughed, and Asher shook his head.

"Nope. I'm not asking. I don't even want to know."

Chapter Twenty-Five

The hour for homework—we actually stretched it closer to two—helped like everything. I'd been afraid I'd start getting behind again, but now I could relax and enjoy the evening without worrying.

As I followed Levi down the stairs, I took a deep breath and reached for a cigarette—my usual way to unwind after studying. I had it halfway to my mouth when the look on Levi's face stopped me, and I remembered in a flash that most church people didn't smoke.

"Sorry, I—" I felt embarrassed for some reason I couldn't explain. "I guess I—shouldn't do that here, right? It'd probably get you in trouble, wouldn't it?"

"We don't care about that." Asher was standing at the bottom of the stairs, and I knew he'd seen it, too. "We don't smoke, but if you need to, just take it outside, please."

His tone was the same as it had been before, but his eyes were sad, and he put a hand on Levi's shoulder as he reached him.

Levi took a shaky breath and didn't look at me, but the first glimpse I'd had of his face still confused me. It wasn't just disapproval or disgust—I could've sworn it was pain.

"Is it—that big a deal?" I asked, and Asher smiled a little.

"There's a lot of reasons we don't smoke, and we're happy to give them to you. But for us—it's personal. Our grandparents smoked, and so did our mom when she was a teenager, before she gave her life to Jesus. Even for a while afterward. She quit not long after she met Dad. She, uh—she died of lung cancer three years ago."

"From the smoking?"

"Doctors said quitting improves your chances a lot, but—it can't totally reverse things."

I'd heard stuff like that in health class, but it'd all sounded like scare tactics. I'd never known anybody that'd actually had it happen.

"I'm sorry." I looked down at my shoes, feeling more uncomfortable than ever.

"It was awful." Levi's voice was choked with tears. "The doctors said it was—really aggressive. She—she only lived three months."

I kept my head down, but all of a sudden, he turned and looked straight up at me.

"It's not all about Mom, DaVonte. I just—I don't want anything like that—to happen to you."

The honesty in his voice and his eyes hit me like a bucket of water to the face, and I sat down suddenly on the stairs. I'd been afraid they were upset with me for breaking one of their rules, but this went way beyond that. They weren't mad or disgusted or disappointed—they were scared for me. Very few people in my life had ever cared about me like that.

"You all right?" Asher asked, and I could hear the concern in his voice.

I nodded, then realized I was still holding the cigarette. In one way, I wanted it more than ever, but in another way, I knew I couldn't do it. Not to them. I stuck it back in my pocket, then stood up, walked down the stairs, and dropped the whole pack in the trash can.

Asher's smile got a little deeper, and Levi looked up with a hopeful gasp.

"You're quitting?"

"I'll think about it. Probably." It was a big decision, and somehow I knew I needed to be sure before I promised.

Levi's forehead wrinkled, but Asher nodded.

"Count the cost before you put your hand to the plow. If you decide to quit, remember, we're here for you—all of us. And Dad or I would be happy to talk with you if you want to find out more. But even if you don't quit, it won't change the way we feel about you. We still care; that's why we're saying it."

"I know." I tried to swallow the lump in my throat.

Levi turned away and rubbed his eyes with his sleeve, and at the same minute, the front door opened, and his dad walked in.

"Everything all right?" He looked at Levi, then me, then Asher. Asher's laugh was a little forced, but I knew he meant it for real.

"Everything's fine. We were just discussing smoking."

Understanding flashed across his dad's face, and his eyebrows went up a little.

"Interesting topic. What's the consensus?"

"I'm thinking of quitting." I glanced up at his eyes and saw even more compassion than I'd seen in Asher's. He didn't say anything else, just put a hand on my shoulder and squeezed, and I felt so warm and safe and cared for that tears suddenly pricked the backs of my eyes. Asher cleared his throat.

"Dinner's ready whenever you are."

Mr. Allison nodded, and Levi and I both laughed—really shaky laughs—for no reason at all. Once we'd started, though, neither of us could stop, and I knew we must look ridiculous, standing there and laughing hysterically at nothing with tears running down our cheeks.

"Dinner sounds great," I got out finally, wiping at the tears that hadn't all been from laughter.

"Even if it's Asher's cooking." Levi sounded dangerously close to going off again, and I knew if he did, I wouldn't be able to stop myself. I clamped a hand over his mouth and almost had him in a headlock when I felt the knot on the back of his head. I let go with a gasp.

"I'm sorry, man. I forgot—I—"

"It's fine. It's fine." Levi gasped for breath. "I'm all right. Honest."

"Not hurt? Maybe. All right? Highly doubtful." Asher surveyed us suspiciously, and we both snickered. His dad put a hand up.

"Don't start them again. Please." He smiled as he nodded toward the table. "Come on, let's eat. And I have something I want to talk to you about. I think we may have the start of a plan, but I'm definitely going to need your help—both of you."

Chapter Twenty-Six

"Tell me why we're doing this again?" Levi took a deep breath and flexed his fingers as he studied the spray-painted wall behind the basketball courts.

"Because your dad said we can't just be different. We have to be accessible. People have to know we're still real and normal and want to be around them."

Levi took a deep breath.

"I don't think either of us qualifies as normal."

DaVonte laughed.

"Well, at least do your best impression. You know you're not coming down here without me or Asher or somebody. But I'm gonna try to get you some more protection when you are down here. Come on." He opened a door and nodded to Levi to follow.

Levi blinked and squinted his eyes as he stepped into the dusky building.

"What is this place?"

"Used to be the rec center. Still is, I guess, only the city doesn't fund it any more. Ms. Sondra runs it. She's the one I want you to meet."

The boys' footsteps echoed in the nearly empty building as they followed the faint sound of voices to a room near the back where three small glitter-covered girls were painting what might have been rainbows. When DaVonte poked his head in, the gray-haired woman at the large desk in the corner hoisted herself to her feet, picked up a cane, and made her way over to the door.

"Well, DaVonte Jones? Come on, now. You want something, or you wouldn't come looking for me."

At the sound of her sharp voice, Levi took a step back, but DaVonte motioned him forward.

"Ms. Sondra, this is my friend Levi. Levi Allison." He turned to Levi. "She likes last names. You'll get used to that." Another turn back to the older woman. "He's gonna start hanging out down here with me some, so I thought he'd better get to know you."

"Come here, young man." Ms. Sondra's eyes narrowed, and she beckoned with her finger.

Levi swallowed hard and took a step closer, and as Ms. Sondra studied him, her frown grew deeper.

"Now, what's a nice uptown boy like you want to come 'hang out' in a place like this for?"

"I—" Levi rubbed a finger along his watch. "Like DaVonte said—we're friends—and I—I want to meet some of his other friends. I don't—I don't want my friends to be all like me—or to have to come to where I am."

He was starting to tremble, and DaVonte clapped him on the shoulder and held out his fist.

"Fish sticks."

"Joan of Arc." Levi took a deep breath and copied the motion, and Ms. Sondra tapped her cane impatiently.

"Boys and their slang! DaVonte Jones, when will you learn to speak so you're understood?"

"I understood him." Levi grinned as he looked up at his friend, and Ms. Sondra huffed.

"Well, that makes one of us. Now, if there is nothing else, I am teaching a class."

"I promised to keep him safe while he's down here." DaVonte looked into her eyes, and an unspoken message seemed to pass between them. "And he's never coming after dark. But if he ever needs anything, I'm telling him to come to you."

"Hmmph." Ms. Sondra turned back to study Levi again. "I suppose if you stick with DaVonte, nothing much'll happen to you." She reached into the pocket of her smock and took out a small card. "Now, don't you call this number unless you mean it. Ms. Sondra don't stand for no shenanigans, hear me?"

Levi nodded with wide eyes as the woman poked the card into his hand.

"Well, go on, take it! I haven't got all day. I have a class to teach."

She shuffled back to the desk, and DaVonte jerked his head for Levi to follow him out.

"What was that all about?" Levi lowered his voice to a whisper, and DaVonte stopped and turned a serious face toward him.

"Guard that card like gold. Ms. Sondra means what she says. If anything ever happens down here—to you or to me while I'm with you—it won't, but if it does—call that number or get to the rec center right away. Ms. Sondra's better than the cops down here. If you're with her, you're safe—got it?"

"You sure I'm safe from her?" Levi gave him a doubtful look, and DaVonte laughed as they headed for the door.

"Trust me, her bark's bad, and her bite's worse, but she only bites if you deserve it. She knows right off who needs protected and who needs protected from, and she's got you sized up straight. Trust me—and trust her."

"That's what you meant about more protection?"

"Part of it."

"What's the rest?"

"For starters, we're playing basketball."

Levi closed his eyes.

"Do I have to?"

"Yup."

"I am really not good at basketball." Levi looked up pleadingly, and DaVonte grinned.

"I'm not that good either. It doesn't matter. We're just gonna play."

DaVonte picked up a ball and dribbled a few times before bouncing it toward Levi, who missed by inches and had to chase it across the court. A few shrill whistles sounded from the kids gathered outside the chain-link fence.

"Are you sure I have to do this?" Levi's face was red as he trotted back with the ball.

"Positive. But since no one here wants to let us play—" DaVonte scanned the courts already in use, whose occupants hadn't looked once in their direction. "We'll make it one-on-one. Know the rules?"

"No."

"You'll learn. First to eleven. Take it out past the three-point line. You go first."

Chapter Twenty-Seven

It had to be the shortest game of one-on-one on record. Not only could Levi not shoot to save his life, he could barely catch my returns, and his dribbling skills were almost non-existent. The laughter and hoots from the sidelines, including most of the guys who'd been playing on the other courts, were almost deafening.

After a few minutes, I decided I was only making things worse, so I stopped giving him chances and just put him out of his misery. When my eleventh point cleared the hoop, Levi dropped down next to the fence and took a long gulp of water from one of the bottles I'd brought.

"I told you." He gasped for air and took another long drink. "There's a difference between 'not really good at basketball' and 'really not good at basketball.'"

"Hey, I believe you." I couldn't help laughing. "I'm completely convinced that you're absolutely no good at basketball."

"Good. Maybe you'll listen to me next time."

"Hey, D!" Reese Mason was walking toward us, a wide smirk on his face. "We got it figured out—why you're so friendly with the bridgers now. It's 'cause you finally found someone you can beat at the hoop!"

Everyone else erupted in cheers and catcalls, and I pretended to glare at him.

"Want me to rub your face in those words?"

"You and who? Your little, uh, water boy here?"

I rolled my eyes.

"Nah, he's done for today. Me and any two you pick. Three on three. Five minutes. If you think you're up to it."

"We'll take you apart."

"Yeah, we'll just see about that."

"Five minutes." Reese walked back toward the sidelines, and I turned to Levi, grinning.

"Plan B accomplished. Not quite the way I planned it, but maybe better."

"That was plan B?"

"Not plan B, I guess. Step two."

"Step two was making me look completely ridiculous?"

I shook my head.

"Step two was getting them to talk to me again. Even if it's just to grind my face in the dirt when I lose, which I will. The point is, they're talking to me and they're letting me play. See how huge that is?"

"Yeah, glad I could help." He still didn't sound totally convinced, but it didn't matter.

"Now, plan C. Step three. Whatever. Come on." I pulled him to his feet, and he shook his head.

"Is this going to be anything like the last one? Because I think I'm done."

"Nothing like. You said you play chess, right?"

"Yeah." He looked a little more hopeful as he followed me off the court.

"Any good?"

"Not bad."

"Perfect. There's someone else I want you to meet."

"I don't know if I'm up to this." Levi's steps started to drag again, and I stopped.

"Listen, I was watching you while we were playing. You were awful, you were embarrassed, you had dozens of people watching and laughing at you, but you weren't sick. Why?"

Levi blinked and shook his head.

"I—I don't know."

"My guess—you had something to do with your mind and your hands. You were so busy playing—or trying to play—"

He elbowed me in the side, and I laughed.

"The point is, you were busy doing something, and you didn't have time to be nervous. That's why I want you to try this. If it doesn't work, that's fine. Come get me, and we'll call Asher. Okay?"

"What, are you a therapist now?" Levi squinted at me, and I grinned.

"Maybe I should be. Just one rule. Don't leave this bench unless you're coming back to the courts. I can see you from there. Don't go anywhere else, or with anyone, and I mean anyone—unless it's Ms. Sondra. She ever tells you to do anything, you do it and don't ask questions. Got it?"

Levi nodded quickly, and I led him to the table where Elroy Morse always set up his chessboard.

"Hey, Mr. Elroy!" I gave him a high five—still his favorite greeting, even though he pretended to keep up with the times.

"Hey, D, where you been, man?"

"Everywhere, man. It's wild. Tell you sometime. Look, I need a favor."

"Yeah?"

"Yeah. I came to play basketball, but the kid here doesn't play—I mean really doesn't play." I shook my head, and Levi rolled his eyes.

"Do you have to rub it in?"

I winked at him but kept talking to Elroy.

"I said I'd keep an eye on him, but I gotta have a place to put him, and this isn't quite as, you know, physical."

Levi's scowl was getting deeper, but he didn't speak the language down here the way I did. I hoped he'd forgive me when I explained it later.

"So what you need's a babysitter."

'Come on, man." I lifted my hands. "Just play the game with him. You're always looking for new blood, right?"

"Don't remember the last time I played a bridger." Elroy squinted up at Levi. "What's he down here for, anyway?"

"Trying to—make new friends." Levi swallowed hard and looked at me, and I nodded. "I don't want people to—to put me in a box. I want to be—different."

"Come on, D, what's this really about?" Elroy eyed me suspiciously, and I grinned.

"Starting a rebellion, man. Wouldn't you love to see the faces on the kids at school? Levi'll tell you about it. While you're playing." I thumped Levi on the shoulder. "He plays, you talk. He starts interrogating, you clam up, right?"

He shot me a pleading look, and I held out my fist.

"Trust me."

"Fish sticks." Levi took a deep breath and tipped his fist toward mine.

"Joan of Arc. You got this, man. I'll be right there if you need me. Go get 'em."

Chapter Twenty-Eight

"So how'd it go?" Asher eyed the boys curiously as they climbed into the car.

"Ask him." Levi glanced warily at DaVonte.

"Knocked it out of the park."

"And just about knocked me along with it."

DaVonte shook his head and closed his eyes.

"Sorry, man. I wasn't trying to get rid of you. It's just the way we talk—the way I knew Elroy would listen to."

"Yeah, I got that." Levi nudged his shoulder gently. "I just still don't see what we really accomplished down here—besides getting me a place to run if I need it."

"That's because you don't know 'down here.' Today was huge. Believe me."

Levi sighed.

"Yeah, you keep saying that. And I'm trying to. But can't you explain any of it?"

"I'll try. Look, we need two things if we're gonna be down here, right? You to be safe—because they will know you don't belong—and them to quit ignoring us."

"Okay. So Ms. Sondra accomplishes the first, and the basketball mess takes care of the second. But what's chess got to do with anything?"

"It's both." DaVonte grinned. "You want to know who you were playing with?"

"Mr. Elroy?" Levi shrugged. "So what?"

"So that was Elroy 'The Lion' Morse. I know that doesn't mean anything to you, but it means everything in Graveside. He's the one-time king of the Blades—that's one of our biggest gangs. Everybody down here knows him. More important, everybody down here listens to him."

"You made me play chess with a gang leader?" Levi's face had gone white.

"Ex-gang leader. And that's exactly why I didn't tell you. Don't worry—he's gone straight ever since his third prison term."

Levi slumped back against the seat.

"Are you sure that was—safe?" Asher's eyes were wide in the rearview mirror.

"He was out in the open in the middle of the park, and in full view of the basketball court where I was. As long as he stayed put and didn't go off with anyone, he was fine. And you agreed to that, right, Levi?"

Levi nodded slowly, drawing a shuddering breath.

"Listen, I'm not gonna go around introducing you to random gang members." DaVonte sighed. "The guys listen to Elroy. You played him—didn't beat him—but played him well enough that it was a good game. He likes that—a lot. And he likes you. He likes truth, even if he doesn't understand it, and he sees that in you. I mean, maybe he can even meet Jesus someday. Wouldn't that be awesome?"

His eyes shone for a minute, and Asher blinked hard. Then DaVonte shook himself back to the present.

"But the point today was—he likes you. Number one, all the guys are gonna think twice about messing with a kid Elroy likes. That's safety. Number two, some of them are gonna be willing to dig deeper and try to find out what he likes about you. That's acceptance—or at least not ignoring. Do you see it now?"

"Yeah." Levi nodded slowly. "Yeah, I guess."

"I did talk to your dad about it first—tell him what I wanted to do."

"You did?" Levi looked up in surprise, and Asher breathed a sigh of relief.

"Kid, you almost gave me a heart attack."

"And I wouldn't have left you alone if I didn't think you could handle it." DaVonte punched Levi gently on the shoulder. "And you did. You were great. I knew you could do it."

Levi blew out a long breath.

"Right. So, Asher, my therapist here tells me that all I have to do is find something to do with my hands when I have to give a report in class, and I'll be fine."

"What?" Asher shot him a puzzled look, and Levi shook his head.

"Never mind."

"I didn't say that." DaVonte elbowed him in the ribs, and Levi squirmed away. "I'm not sure how you'd make that work, but—it's really not a bad idea, if you could do it."

"Yeah, sure. When they start making accommodations for 'speech-phobia', I'll just request that I can—try to play basketball."

DaVonte shot him a sideways glance.

"You really were awful."

"Yeah." Levi sighed, then suddenly chuckled. "Yeah, I was, wasn't I?" He put his head back on the seat and howled with laughter, and DaVonte drew a long sigh of relief.

"So this end is set to go." Asher glanced back at them as Levi's laughter subsided. "You guys ready for tomorrow?"

"I feel like tomorrow's not going to be as—easy—as today." Levi pursed his lips, and DaVonte's eyebrows shot up.

"You feel like? You're the fish in water tomorrow. How do you think I feel?"

"Pray, guys." Asher shook his head. "Our church needs a wake-up call as badly as Graveside, and in either place, the Lord's the only one that can do it. We're picking you up at nine tomorrow, DaVonte?"

DaVonte nodded.

"And you've okayed it with your friend at the pawnshop?"

"He's still—not thrilled about it—but he says he'll try it once."

"We'll convince him."

"I'm still not sure why you guys are doing this." DaVonte shook his head. "It's not part of the plan or anything—except maybe this one time."

"Because we want you at church—plan or no plan. If the four of us work for half your hours, that cuts the number of Sundays down by half, too. Right?"

"Yeah—if you convince him you're worth it."

"That must have been some debt you owed him." Levi looked up quizzically, and DaVonte pressed his lips together, then smiled suddenly.

"Yeah. Yeah, it sure was. You have no idea how big, and neither did I—'til now."

Chapter Twenty-Nine

True to his word, Mr. Allison was at my door at nine Sunday morning. I'd waited outside for fifteen minutes before he got there, since I'd forgotten to ask him not to honk the horn for me. That would've been an awful start to getting them off on a good foot in the neighborhood.

I took one look at their clothes when I climbed into the car and closed my eyes, wanting to just go back to bed.

"What's wrong?" Levi nudged my shoulder.

"Look, this is the best I got, man. I mean, if I knew I was gonna stick out this bad—"

"DaVonte." Mr. Allison waited 'til I looked up at the mirror. "Church is not about clothes. If you'd like to clean up, dress up a little bit for Sundays, then we can help with that. But I'd rather you came in a chicken suit—if that was all you had—than to stay away because of your clothes. Understand?"

The chicken suit made me smile—he'd probably meant it that way. He smiled, too, then his eyes were serious again.

"Not everyone at church today—maybe not most people—are going to feel the way I do about it. That's one of the things we need to work on. The church is full of people—real, flawed people like you and me—and it's far from perfect. But God's not finished with us yet. You know how God feels about you, you know the truth of who you are in Him, and no one can take that away from you. All right?"

I swallowed hard and nodded.

"Would it help if I change into my work clothes?" Levi nodded toward a faded pair of jeans on the floor—probably the ones he'd brought for cleaning the pawnshop that afternoon. The look on his face said it wouldn't be easy for him, but he'd do it to help me out. I smiled.

"Nah, man, go ahead. This is your fish in water day, remember? Don't shock them too bad, or they might not listen. Can you tell me how this is gonna go again?"

Levi grinned and went back over the program—the service, he called it—for probably the fifth time, finishing the same way he always did.

"Don't worry. You'll be sitting next to me. I'll nudge you if you forget."

If he only knew how little I really got of what he was trying to explain. I bent the Bible Mr. Allison had given me back and forth in my hands and turned my eyes out the window.

"Hey," Levi whispered, and I looked up. "That's my thing."

"What?"

"Fidgeting like that." He grinned as he put his hand on the Bible. "Don't be nervous. You're going to do fine. It's not like we're making you play basketball—I mean, collect the offering or anything."

"Yeah, thanks." I turned away, and he touched my shoulder.

"Hey, man. Trust me."

He held out his fist, and I grinned a little shakily. So this was how it felt.

"Fish sticks?" I tipped my fist toward his, and he nodded.

"Joan of Arc—and better."

"That has got to be the strangest code anyone's ever come up with." Asher's forehead wrinkled as he watched us, and we both grinned.

"It's a long story," Levi said.

"It'd have to be."

"Okay, prayers, people." Mr. Allison glanced back at us as he stopped the car in front of the gray stone church I'd seen so many times from the bus window. "Let's be ready—and see what God's going to do."

Chapter Thirty

"Did you see that?" Peyton's eyes flashed as he strode up to Sam and Jodie Walker. "That deadbeat kid sitting right up in front with the pastor's family. Who does he think he is?"

"Is he coming to our class?" Jodie clutched her purse tighter and shivered.

"If he does, my parents are going to hear about it." Peyton shook his head decidedly. "We don't know anything about this kid. Who knows what kind of stuff he's bringing in here? It's not safe. There's no way."

"I mean—I guess they need the gospel down there, too." Sam shifted uncomfortably, and Peyton sighed.

"Sure. Of course they do. So someone should take it down there. Not bring them up here. It's not safe; it's not respectful; it's distracting. There's a right way and a wrong way to work with people like that, and this is not the right way."

"So what do we do if he is in class?" Sam pursed his lips and frowned.

"Talk to your parents. Tell them our concerns. They can take it to Pastor, and he can deal with it. Hey, and pass the word to the other kids. This is our church, too, and we need to feel safe here. If they don't, they need to tell their parents about it. Okay?"

"What about Levi?" Jodie asked, and Peyton shook his head sadly.

"I don't know what's happened with him. You've seen him at school. He won't even sit with us anymore. Give him a wide berth until he gets his act together. Look, talk to as many kids as you can before class, okay?"

Sam and Jodie nodded, and Peyton headed for a knot of teenagers standing near the back of the sanctuary.

By the time Mrs. Ellis rang the bell for Sunday school, the classroom was a beehive of whispers and mumbles, and the tiny, white-haired woman had to raise her voice to be heard over the commotion.

"Class, please. Class. I must have your attention."

The murmur quieted but continued steadily.

"Class!"

"Hey, guys!" Peyton stood and eyed his classmates with a frown. "Mrs. Ellis is talking."

The room was still almost instantly, and their teacher breathed a sigh of relief.

"Thank you, Peyton. Now, class, we must begin our study immediately. Pastor Allison has a special message for you at the end of our time, so for prayer requests—" She paused and hesitated.

Peyton shot a glance at Natalie, who raised her hand.

"Mrs. Ellis, if people write their requests on the board after class, I can take a picture and text it to everyone."

"Wonderful, Natalie." Mrs. Ellis beamed. "Everyone, please write your requests on the board, and then make sure that Natalie has your 'text.'"

A few of the kids snickered, but Peyton silenced them with a look, and Mrs. Ellis turned to the blackboard.

"Now, who remembers where we left off in Joshua?"

"Chapter nine?" a voice from the back volunteered.

"Very good. Peyton, will you read the first five verses for us?"

The class went on as usual, the only exception being the frequent looks cast toward the back corner, where Levi and DaVonte sat in the two farthest chairs. Finally, just as Mrs. Ellis finished writing the last point and laid down her chalk, there was a knock at the door, and Pastor Allison stepped inside, greeting her and the class with a warm smile.

"Class." Mrs. Ellis beamed as she turned to face them. "As I told you earlier, Pastor Allison has a special message for you all. Please join me in welcoming him."

The teens clapped politely, then waited, their expressions showing varying degrees of interest. Peyton leaned forward, frowning slightly. Levi drew a deep breath, and DaVonte tensed.

"I'd like to tell you a story today." Pastor Allison sat down on a corner of the desk and nodded to Mrs. Ellis to take her own chair. "And it's a story that involves one of our own—Brett Martens—who some of you know was released from the hospital this week. Unfortunately, he's still resting and couldn't be with us today, but he's given me permission to share this story with all of you, in the hopes that it will touch you the way it did him.

"Brett was out running past the bridge near River Street two Wednesdays ago—not a wise choice, although he didn't know it at the time—when he was attacked in an alley by a number of young men—at least some of whom have now been arrested."

DaVonte shot a glance at Levi, who nodded and mouthed, "Tell you later."

"Brett was robbed, beaten, stabbed in the stomach, and left to die."

A shudder went around the room, and Pastor Allison nodded.

"But in God's amazing providence, another boy was near the alley that night—one who was born and raised in Graveside. This young man knew nothing of God except what had been said in his hearing as a child by a stranger who he never saw again. But what he heard was this: 'God cares about you, me, and everyone.'

"Now, any of you who attend Woodbridge know how deep the divide in your school is. You know how most of the kids in your neighborhoods feel about the kids from Graveside, and you know how most of them feel about you. But when this boy saw Brett lying there, knowing full well where he'd come from, he knew that if that 'everyone' meant him, then it meant Brett, too. And he is the reason Brett is alive today. DaVonte, will you come up here, please?"

DaVonte gave Levi one last look, then slowly stood and made his way up to Pastor Allison.

"Young people, I want you to take a good look and then think about this. If you saw DaVonte bleeding in an alley, what would be your response? Would any of you stop? Think of everything you know about God and His Word, and then ask yourselves the question: 'Does it make a difference in my life?'

"Would God's love compel you—you who know Him, who love Him—to stop and help a stranger the way DaVonte did? And if not, then maybe you need to step back and re-think what you know, what you truly believe about God's love.

"DaVonte knew one thing, and only one, but that one thing compelled him to action. Is what you know about God collecting dust on your shelves like a trophy? Or is it living and breathing within you? Does it make a difference in your lives?"

Pastor Allison paused for a moment, and the silence was unbroken except for shuffling feet and a few audible sniffs.

"Now I'd like to offer you an opportunity—an opportunity to put God's love into practice."

Suddenly, the door flew open, and the church secretary thrust her head in, flushed and breathless.

"Pastor, there's a man on the phone, and I can't understand him, but he says it's urgent! You need to come right away!"

"Sarah—" Pastor Allison hesitated, closed his eyes briefly, then nodded. "If you'll all just please wait here for a few minutes, I'll be back as soon as I can. Think about what I've said." He turned and followed the secretary out the door.

Chapter Thirty-One

There was silence for a long minute after the pastor had gone, and Levi sat on the edge of his chair, his head bent over his hands, his lips moving silently. Suddenly, there was a stir in the front row, and he raised his eyes to find Peyton facing the class.

"Guys." Peyton shook his head with a look of pain. "You know how much I respect our pastor, but in this case, I think he's crossed the line. Sure, we're all glad about Brett, but is he really telling us to follow the example of an unbeliever? What happened to walking 'not in the counsel of the ungodly'? I mean, shouldn't we be listening to what God's Word says, not basing our lives on somebody who doesn't even know the Lord?"

There was a murmur of assent from several voices.

"And telling us that whole story—that's just manipulation. He's working on our feelings to try to get us to buy into this 'opportunity.' I'm not saying he's doing it on purpose. He's passionate. That's great. But the things we're passionate about aren't always the things God wants us to focus on. That's why we have a church board. New ideas are supposed to go through them first, not come straight to us. These things need to be prayed over, planned, financed. Especially if it's going to involve Graveside. Pastor's new in town. He doesn't know all the dangers down there. There's a lot of safety issues I just don't think he's considered."

Peyton paused and sighed.

"And you know Pastor doesn't know our hearts. Whether we'd stop for a stranger, or if we were even supposed to, he can't just assume that. That's between us and God, and He can work on us if we need it. If nothing else, before we just sign on to what he wants us to do, I think we definitely need to talk to our parents first. Have them talk to the board. Make sure we've got everything in order, and this isn't just a dangerous sideroad. We have to be sure as a church that we're keeping our priorities straight."

Heads nodded all over the class, and Peyton smiled slightly as he turned to DaVonte, who stood motionless in the front of the classroom, staring at his shoes.

"I think you'd better sit down now. This is a house of worship, not a rock concert."

"No."

At the single word from the back of the room, everyone's heads turned. Levi stood next to his chair, fists clenched and cheeks burning.

"You're wrong, Peyton. And I'm not listening anymore. Whatever he didn't know before, DaVonte's a brother in Christ now, and he has as much right to be here as anyone. Even if he wasn't, he still has a right to be here—anyone does—to come and hear about God. 'And how shall they hear without a preacher?' If you can quote Scripture, I can do it, too—only I'm going to do it right. 'He who says he is in the light, and hates his brother, is in darkness.' That was Dad's point—not some cheap mind game.

"You want biblical examples?" Levi held up his Bible and shook his head. "It's full of them—people doing just what DaVonte did. Rahab and the spies? How much did she know about God? How about 'love your enemies'? And Dad did go through the board. Brett's dad changed his mind—and a bunch of others. Everything he's talking about today is fully approved. And besides that—"

Levi paused and swallowed hard.

"I don't know all your hearts, but I know my own. And Brett's story—that was my story, too—only you didn't hear my part of it. I was on River Street that night. I saw him. You guys, I wasn't even a stranger. I was a friend—a friend who should've stopped—and instead I turned and ran."

"That's great, Levi. Everyone isn't you." There was a fine edge of scorn in Peyton's voice as he faced his opponent. "Don't think you know what we would do, just because you got scared and ran away."

"No. Peyton, no." Natalie's voice trembled as she rose suddenly from her seat. Peyton glared at her, but she didn't turn away. "I kept quiet because I thought you felt as bad as I did. But I'm not letting you say that about Levi—not when we were just as bad—or worse."

She turned to look slowly around the room.

"We were there, too—on River Street—driving to church. We got stopped at that exact alley, and we saw him. We didn't know who it was, but—we didn't stop." With a deep breath, she faced her brother again. "Levi ran because he was scared—and there was a lot to be scared of. We didn't stop because you were in a hurry to get to your sermon, and I didn't want you to leave me. So which is worse?"

She shook her head slowly.

"I trust Pastor Allison, and more than that, I trust God. And I'm going to start listening to Him, not you." With a sudden movement, she turned on her heel. "I'm with you, Levi. What does your dad want us to do?"

Levi's face had turned the color of chalk, and he clutched the back of a chair for support. His whole body trembled, but he made an effort to speak.

"Trip to—Diamond Cove—August. For anyone—anyone in high school." His hand shook as he wiped at the beads of sweat on his forehead. "Meeting at River Park—Saturday—one P.M. Talk it up at school—tell us if you need a ride."

DaVonte took a step toward him, but at that instant, the door opened, and Pastor Allison entered the room again. Levi gave a gasp that was almost a sob and rushed out the back way.

"Everything all right?" Pastor Allison's brow creased as he looked around at the flushed, excited faces, Peyton and Natalie still standing, and Mrs. Ellis sitting white and bewildered in her chair.

DaVonte gave a shaky grin.

"I think it is now."

"We're ready, Pastor," Natalie spoke up quietly as she took her seat again. "What was it you wanted to tell us?"

Pastor Allison glanced once more at DaVonte, who nodded.

"Go ahead. I'll check on Levi."

With a nod of thanks, Pastor Allison sat down on the desk again, and DaVonte slipped out the door.

He found Levi leaning against a wall in the restroom, breathing heavily and wiping his face with a wet paper towel.

"Some hero, huh?" Levi offered a wan smile, and DaVonte sank down next to him on the floor.

"Are you kidding? What you just did up there took way more guts for you than anything I ever did—for you or Brett or anybody."

"Bet Joan of Arc never got sick in the middle of a battle." Levi closed his eyes, and DaVonte put a hand on his shoulder.

"You can't know that—you're guessing. Bet she was scared, too. Why wouldn't she be? But who cares? And besides, it wasn't the middle. You held out as long as you had to. I can't believe you really did it—talked that long in front of the whole class."

"I didn't even notice at first." Levi swallowed hard and took a deep breath. "It had to be God—most of it. I didn't even think, just—talked. It wasn't 'til after Natalie—I sort of slowed down—realized what I was doing."

"And even after that, you didn't give up. You could've left right then—made them wait for your dad—let that Peyton kid start in again. But you didn't. I think Joan of Arc would be proud. I know Jesus is."

"I'm sorry for what he said about you."

"No worries." DaVonte cracked a slight smile. "Flawed people, right? I guess we should probably pray for him, too."

"You're getting good at this." Levi gave him the shadow of a grin.

"I had a good teacher."

"Do me a favor and don't mention food for a while?" Levi tipped his fist toward his friend, and DaVonte's smile widened as he answered the signal.

"Joan of Arc all the way, man. Joan of Arc—or better."

Chapter Thirty-Two

I sat on the front row of the bleachers between Levi and Brett the next Saturday. There were only a handful of other kids, but Pastor Allison had expected that. We'd get more interest once they saw we were really serious, he said.

I had to hand it to him—he'd picked a great way to start. Diamond Cove was the best amusement park around and far enough away that it was a real treat, even to the rich kids. The idea had everyone talking—even if most of the kids still thought it was a joke.

Ms. Sondra shuffled by, and her eyes went straight to Asher, sitting on the other side of Levi.

"Aren't you a little old for high school, young man?"

"You'll need chaperones, won't you?" Asher grinned back at her, and her eyes narrowed.

"Mmm-hm. And who's chaperoning the chaperones?"

Asher crossed his heart with such an innocent look that I almost laughed, and Ms. Sondra glared at him for a few more seconds before she turned toward the folding chairs sitting in the grass.

"They'll get along great," I whispered to Levi, and he smiled.

Not a whole lot had changed in the last week. Levi and I still ate alone at the front table, although a few kids had stopped by to ask questions—mostly about the trip. Brett was finally back at school, but his head was still way too sensitive to noise to join us. From what I could tell, most of his old crowd would've shipped him off there in a hurry if they could—he sure wasn't keeping quiet about the way God had changed his life.

Natalie from the church class was sitting on the back row of the bleachers with little Amy Song, and I'd heard they'd taken our table at first lunch on Friday. Amy lived in the little Chinese grocery on 6th, and none of us counted her real Graveside, but that didn't matter. She was still 'everyone' and probably needed a place to belong even more than the rest of us. A few other kids from the church had shown up. Peyton wasn't one of them.

One or two guys from across the bridge that Levi didn't know from church were sitting around looking curious, along with a few Graveside kids that Ms. Sondra kept a special eye on. A few others hung around by the back fence but wouldn't come up to the bleachers. Jamal was one of them—I'd hoped he'd be there, especially after the invitation that'd been left with a new pair of sneakers outside his apartment. That had been Brett's work—him and his parents.

Pastor Allison said Brett's dad was a changed man. He'd never thought the church owed much of anything to Graveside, but now he was bringing all kinds of people around to the pastor's way of thinking. Not that this trip was a church event—it was better that way, they said—but I guess just the permission to talk about it to the church kids was huge.

It was one o'clock, and Pastor Allison stood up and thanked us all for coming to the "first informational meeting" for the trip to Diamond Cove. He reminded us that this trip was for anyone and asked us to pass the word, even to kids outside our school.

"Final sign-ups will be due the first of July. Anyone who wants to join after that will need special permission from Ms. Sondra." Pastor Allison nodded toward Ms. Sondra, who sat next to him, and I grinned. Ms. Sondra could smell the difference between a real excuse and a good sob story a mile off.

"In the meantime, we need to start getting the money together right away." Pastor Allison smiled around at us, but his eyes had the spark that meant he knew he was about to shock us. "But the money for this trip is going to be a little—different. Any money you bring in, whether it's through donations or fundraisers, goes to the group, not to you. That means if we can't pay for everyone, no one goes."

There were a few gasps from the rich kids.

"We've got three months before sign-ups close and another month after that. That should be plenty of time to raise the money. And if we get enough people, we'll qualify for a group rate, which will mean the price goes down."

That was a great way to get kids to bring their friends. I glanced at Levi, and he grinned and nodded. One of the church girls raised her hand.

"But what if some of us are raising money, and other people just sign up and don't help? That's not fair."

"That's true." Pastor Allison smiled. "Which is why we're requiring that everyone bring in at least fifty dollars or attend at least four fundraisers. Any exceptions will have to be approved by Ms. Sondra."

Brett sighed, and I nudged him gently.

"Don't worry. Ms. Sondra's already approved at least ten exceptions for you. I saw her watching you earlier."

"Great." Brett frowned a little and rubbed at the gauze pad that'd replaced the bandage on his forehead. "But I'm still coming. I want to pull my weight."

"You will. Just don't pull too hard at first. You got plenty of time—four whole months. Don't try to rush it, or you'll miss the best part."

Pastor Allison was introducing Ms. Sondra for a few words about rules, and I grinned. Sure enough, I could repeat most of it word for word.

We'd "come clean, come sober, or don't bother." She'd better "not so much as smell a weapon" on any of us. Matching t-shirts would be part of the price, and under them she'd "better be able to see your shorts and no more." She'd also have her "stash" on hand—the box of belts and oversized t-shirts she kept at the rec center for anyone whose clothes didn't pass her inspection. If anyone got in trouble, they'd be spending the day on the bus with her, "and let me tell you, child, when I get through with you, you'll wish they'd sent you to prison!"

When Ms. Sondra finished, Pastor Allison asked us again to pass the word and to come back next Saturday with ideas for fundraisers, so we could start planning. The little group broke up quickly, and while Pastor Allison and Ms. Sondra waited for the other kids' rides, Levi, Brett, and I walked down toward the river.

"You know, if you'd told me I'd be doing this three weeks ago, I'd have slapped your face."

"No, you wouldn't." Levi grinned, and I shrugged.

"Laughed in it anyway."

"That I believe."

"God's brought us a long way." Brett's face was a little sad as he looked out over the water. "I wonder how much longer it'll take before we really start making a difference."

I shook my head.

"We're making one already. Look what God did for you—and for me. Baby steps, maybe, but we gotta start somewhere. Even if it's just a bridge between two or three of us, and then ask God to help us build it out."

"Bridgers." Levi's voice sounded far-away, but he suddenly turned toward me. "That's what you guys call us right? Well, I'm thinking maybe that's what God wants us to be. Not like 'far away across the bridge,' but, you know, building bridges. Finding a way over the things that keep us apart."

I looked down toward the real bridge—the one that'd been the dividing line for more years than I could guess.

"If you'd called me that three weeks ago, I really would've slapped you—or at least wanted to bad. It's a hard name to get used to after all that time."

"We don't have to use it." Levi shook his head. "It'd probably give the wrong message anyway. I just want to remember the picture—building bridges in impossible places. Nothing's too hard for God."

"I'll buy that." I nodded slowly. "So what's that make us? Engineers?"

"Not really. God's the engineer. We're just the tools he uses—and I'm glad. I wouldn't want the whole job left up to me."

"Me neither. You know, you're right. Kind of like a construction site. Everything looks like a mess for a long time, like it's not going anywhere. But you can't give up on it—just keep following the plan, and then finally it all comes together."

Levi nodded.

"And we might not even get to see it finished, like the guys who lay the first cables. But if we do the part God gave us, nothing else matters."

"I like that." Brett smiled.

"You're living proof, man." I nudged Levi gently with my elbow, and he grinned back.

"So are you, DaVonte. Believe me, so are you."